THE FORTUNES OF TEXAS

*Follow the lives and loves of a complex family
with a rich history and deep ties
in the Lone Star State*

FORTUNE'S SECRET CHILDREN

*Six siblings discover they're actually part of
the notorious Fortune family and move to
Chatelaine, Texas, to claim their name...while
uncovering shocking truths and life-changing
surprises. Will their Fortunes turn—hopefully, for
the better?*

FORTUNE'S HOLIDAY SURPRISE

*After his best friend perishes in a tragic accident,
financial whiz Arlo Fortune doesn't feel like
celebrating Christmas. But when Carrie Kaplan
arrives to care for his friend's orphaned toddler,
the rancher can't help but be drawn to her. As
Carrie teaches them both about the holiday of
Hanukkah, she might just give Arlo a reason to
celebrate once more.*

Dear Reader,

As a lifelong Jersey girl, the only thing I know about Texas is what I've seen in the movies and hear about in country songs. So when Harlequin asked me to contribute to their Fortunes of Texas series, I was thrilled.

As a writer, I love creating diverse communities where people live, love and laugh together, and where all problems, no matter how big or small, can be overcome. It's essential that my characters find their happily-ever-after and, by doing so, provide hope to my readers.

Hope is especially prevalent during the holidays, and if there were ever two people who needed it more than Arlo Fortune and Carrie Kaplan, well, I haven't met them. Still dealing with the death of his father, Arlo is shocked when his best friend—Carrie's brother-in-law—dies suddenly. Carrie, her newly orphaned niece's guardian, is tasked with teaching her about her Jewish heritage. She's a fish out of water in this tiny Texas town, torn away from the sister she has no idea how to live without.

Welcome back to Chatelaine, where the Fortunes own the biggest ranch in the area. Get ready to celebrate Christmas and Hanukkah as Carrie tries to help Arlo find meaning in the holidays. Stop in at the holiday celebration in the town hall. Admire the decorations and taste the seasonal foods, including the Christmas cookies and Hanukkah bimuelos, the latkes and spiced rum. And if you want to admire the handsome cowboys, well, I'm certainly not going to stop you.

So grab a cup of hot chocolate, turn on the holiday music and dive into this holiday romance. I hope you enjoy Arlo and Carrie's story!

Jennifer Wilck

FORTUNE'S HOLIDAY SURPRISE

JENNIFER WILCK

THE FORTUNES OF TEXAS

Special thanks and acknowledgment are given to
Jennifer Wilck for her contribution to
The Fortunes of Texas: Fortune's Secret Children miniseries.

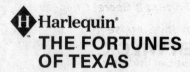

Harlequin®
THE FORTUNES OF TEXAS

Recycling programs for this product may not exist in your area.

ISBN-13: 978-1-335-99676-3

Fortune's Holiday Surprise

Copyright © 2024 by Harlequin Enterprises ULC

Harlequin Enterprises ULC
22 Adelaide St. West, 41st Floor
Toronto, Ontario M5H 4E3, Canada
www.Harlequin.com

Printed in Lithuania

MIX
Paper | Supporting responsible forestry
FSC® C021394

Jennifer Wilck is an award-winning contemporary romance author for readers who are passionate about love, laughter and happily-ever-after. Known for writing both Jewish and non-Jewish romances, she features damaged heroes, sassy and independent heroines, witty banter, yummy food and hot chemistry in her books. She believes humor is the only way to get through the day and does not believe in sharing her chocolate. You can find her at jenniferwilck.com.

Books by Jennifer Wilck

The Fortunes of Texas: Fortune's Secret Children

Fortune's Holiday Surprise

Harlequin Special Edition

Holidays, Heart and Chutzpah

Home for the Challah Days
Matzah Ball Blues
Deadlines, Donuts & Dreidels

Visit the Author Profile page
at Harlequin.com for more titles.

To Debbie & Alyse—thank you for helping this Jersey
girl learn about the thriving Jewish communities
in Texas. I couldn't have written this book without you.

Prologue

Arlo Fortune stared at his best friend's front door and blinked hard. Only a week and a half ago, Isaac Abelman and his wife had died in a freak gas explosion while on a business trip overseas. Arlo had endured a funeral worse than any other he'd attended, including his own father's. And now, seven days later, he'd come to pay a condolence call to Isaac's grieving sister-in-law, someone he barely knew. He pulled at the clasp of his bolero tie and wondered if he should knock on the blue oak door or ring the black iron doorbell.

Once upon a time, he'd opened the door without a care, yelling hello to Isaac, kissing Isaac's wife, Randi, on the cheek and tickling the chin of their toddler daughter, Aviva. Hell, going back even further, to his and Isaac's childhood, he couldn't remember the last time he'd knocked or rung before entering.

But now?

He grimaced and didn't realize anyone was walking behind him until a throat cleared, and a man and a woman said, "Excuse me," before moving past him, walking up the steps to the front porch and opening the door.

Despite the grief that slowed his thoughts and body, Arlo quickened his pace and followed the couple into the house.

He expected Randi to greet him, Aviva on one hip, a grin on her face. Instead, one of his neighbors nodded to him. From the front hall, Arlo glanced into the full living room on the right, filled with murmuring voices and subdued laughter. On his left was the dining room where he and his friend had shared many a meal. Today, the maple table was covered with a white cloth and loaded with platters of food and trays of dessert. More people gathered around it, helping themselves and huddling in groups.

He'd fiddled with his tie so much it probably needed fixing, but the mirror in the front hall was covered, probably a Jewish mourning custom he didn't know, so he smoothed his hand down his front and wandered into the fray.

Snatches of conversation drifted toward him.

"...so sad about the baby."

"...such a freak accident."

"...going to stay here..."

Arlo scanned the room, trying to find someone he knew. He'd never paid a shiva call before, and he didn't know what was expected.

Spotting one of his friends across the room, he started to make his way in his direction when a voice interrupted him.

"Ladies and gentlemen, if everyone could come into the living room for the minyan, please."

Minyan? What was that?

Someone handed him a book, open to the beginning. There was English and Hebrew writing on it, but the book was backward. He frowned. The rabbi he'd seen at the funeral walked to the front of the room and began to read.

The English was meaningful, the Hebrew chanting beautiful, and it brought into focus the importance of being together in this time of grief. As he listened to the prayers murmured around him, he looked at the people in the room.

Many of them were neighbors and townspeople he recognized. Some were people he'd grown up with. Others were strangers to him.

His gaze stopped when it landed on Randi's sister. Arlo remembered her name was Carrie. Isaac had mentioned her occasionally, and he'd seen her at their wedding five years ago, but this was the first time he'd really had time to notice her.

She was pretty, with long dark hair she had twisted up in some kind of knot, big brown eyes filled with sadness and pale skin.

She looked...alone. Despite everyone joining her in mourning, there was a wall around her. He didn't know if it was of her own making or maybe his imagination. But sympathy tugged at him.

In the middle of the service, Aviva began fussing. Carrie reached for her, and he thought he saw fear in her eyes, but he blinked and it was gone.

What must it be like to have parenthood thrust upon you like that? Aviva was adorable. He'd always had a bond with her, but even still, taking care of a two-year-old out of the blue? What kind of life change must that be?

He wanted to go up and reintroduce himself to her, see how she was doing and check on Aviva. But when the service ended, a swarm of people crowded around her, and he was forced to wait. He wandered through the living room into the kitchen, stopping to greet people he knew.

"Terrible tragedy," his friend Jim said. "I talked to him the night before he left. Never thought it would be the last time, though."

Arlo's throat thickened. "Yeah." His voice croaked, and he made a fist with his hand at his side. He hadn't spoken to Isaac since a month before he died, and when he had, they'd argued. He'd had many arguments with his friend, but they'd always made up afterward. This time, they never would. He wanted to scream and shout at the unfairness of it all.

The rabbi walked past him, nodding to those he knew, and approached the table full of food. All of the guests treated him with respect, appropriate for a man of God. Arlo shook his head. How could he believe in a God who left a two-year-old parentless? What possible reason could He have for taking away his best friend and that man's wife? He huffed out a frustrated breath. For that matter, what kind of God took *his* father and left him with more questions than ever before and no way of getting answers?

Nope, he didn't want to interact with the rabbi, no matter how nice of a service he'd led. He turned away from the dining room and ran smack into Carrie.

Reflexively, he reached out to keep from knocking her over.

"Sorry about that." He removed his hat and held out his hand. "Arlo Fortune. Isaac was my best friend. I'm sorry for your loss."

The sorrow he'd seen in her eyes deepened, the dark brown reminding him of his polished leather saddle.

"Thank you." Her voice was soft. "I'm sorry for yours as well."

Something about her expression made him want to continue the conversation, to ask how she was holding up, what she was doing about Aviva, and to offer his assistance, if necessary. But before he put those thoughts into words, another mourner approached. With a tip of his hat, he retreated a step and soon the crowd swallowed her, and he turned and left.

Chapter One

One month later...

Every time Carrie Kaplan walked into her sister's cheery kitchen, her stomach hurt. She'd avoid the room if she could—as a nutritionist and health/wellness writer with syndicated columns across multiple online sites, she was an expert on how to take care of yourself and do what's best for yourself—but this was no longer her sister's kitchen.

The yellow kitchen with white curtains was now hers.

Only a month ago, this had been her sister's house, the place where she lived with her husband and adorable daughter, Aviva. Carrie had packed a weeks' worth of clothes and arrived excited to babysit her niece while they left on a business trip.

Killed tragically in their hotel, they never came home.

Now, as Aviva's guardian and new owner of her sister's house, she faced a life completely different from the one she imagined.

And walking into this kitchen several times a day gave her a stomachache.

"Me hungwy," Aviva said, tapping Carrie's leg.

Despite her sadness, she smiled down at her niece before lifting her to her hip and nuzzling her cheek.

"Well, then, we should feed you," she murmured.

"Yes, pwese."

As she'd done a thousand times since moving in here, Carrie wanted to tell her sister how adorable Aviva was, especially when she used her manners. She blinked back tears as she placed the little girl in her high chair next to the big bay window overlooking the grasslands of the nearby ranches.

Between the cold December weather and the early morning, no one was on the road, other than trucks delivering supplies. If her brother-in-law were still alive, though, he'd be pulling into the driveway with treats from the nearby bakery before heading upstairs to work in his home office. With a sigh, she opened the fridge and pulled out some fruit. In the freezer, she grabbed a frozen waffle and stuck it in the toaster.

"What color plate would you like today?" she asked Aviva. "Pink or orange?"

"Owage."

Carrie cut up the fruit into toddler-sized bites and placed it on the plastic dish. When the waffle popped, she added that to the plate, making sure to cut it up as well. Then she put the breakfast on Aviva's high chair tray, added her sippy cup of milk and sat down next to her.

"Auntie Cawwy eat, too?"

Crap. She wasn't hungry, but she needed to be a good role model.

She smacked her forehead. "Oh, my goodness, I forgot!" She widened her eyes and dropped her jaw, making Aviva giggle.

She grabbed herself a yogurt and spoon and joined her niece at the table.

"What shall we do today, kiddo?"

"Swings!" Aviva gave a wide, toothy grin as she answered with her favorite activity.

"You always say swings."

"Swings!"

Carrie cleaned Aviva's mouth, hands and high chair tray before unstrapping her and placing her on the ground. "First, let's get dressed." She looked down at her own pajama-clad self. She needed to get changed, too.

It had taken her a little while to learn to balance caring for a toddler and herself, but the two of them had developed a routine.

Carrie appreciated routine. It gave her a sense of control and prevented her from curling up in a ball with her grief. And now that she'd sent for her clothes and most of her things back in Albuquerque—even if it was only for the time being—she was starting to feel a little more like herself.

She followed Aviva upstairs to her bedroom. The little girl ran over to her dresser, opened drawers and pulled clothing onto the floor. Carrie stood in the doorway, watching the flurry of activity. After a couple of minutes of marching and bending and tossing, Aviva stood up, triumphant.

"I want to wear this," she said.

Carrie nodded, impressed. Although the items didn't come close to matching, they were weather appropriate. The child had picked a pair of bright orange leggings with a pink and blue tunic top. Once again, she silently thanked her sister for only keeping seasonal clothes within reach.

"You will be one colorful kid," she said, folding up the discarded items and replacing them in the drawers, before helping Aviva to put on her clothes.

When she was dressed, with an orange bow in her hair—

Carrie needed *something* to match—she brought her into the guest room, sat Aviva on the bed with the TV turned on to the latest kiddie show and got herself ready for the day.

A commercial for a store with Christmas sales came on, and with a jolt, Carrie realized Hanukkah was coming, too.

In addition to naming Carrie as Aviva's guardian when she was born, Randi had requested that Carrie help impart Jewish customs and traditions on her niece. At the time, Carrie had been thrilled with the task. She remembered her grandmother lighting the Shabbat candles and reciting the blessings on Friday nights, going to synagogue in their best clothes, and cooking delicious food. She and Randi had grown up with her grandparents, now long dead, and they had shown both Carrie and Randi the importance of Judaism. Carrie had looked forward to celebrating the holidays with her niece.

She'd never planned on being the only one to carry on the tradition, though.

With Hanukkah approximately a month away, Carrie had a lot to prepare for.

Her sister and brother-in-law's bedroom door was shut. No matter how much time Carrie had spent here, and how many of Randi's things she'd gone through, she couldn't make herself tackle their bedroom.

"Mommy Daddy room," Aviva said, rushing over and reaching for the handle. Her little body stretched, but it was just out of her reach.

"That's right, Vivie. Let's go downstairs, though, okay?" Her throat was thick, but she pushed the words through anyway. With Aviva so young, Carrie couldn't explain too much about her parents' deaths, but had relied on some simple storybooks and lots and lots of love to do her best to cushion the impact of their sudden disappearance from her life.

"Otay."

Thank goodness Aviva was so easy.

"Come on, kiddo, let's go outside." The thought of spending all day inside the house, going through her brother-in-law's things, oppressed her. She'd wait until Aviva went down for a nap. In the meantime, it would do them both good to get some fresh air.

After bundling her niece into her jacket and strapping her into her stroller, Carrie walked into downtown Chatelaine.

She laughed to herself. "Downtown Chatelaine" was really just one road with a one-pump gas station at the town line proclaiming "Welcome to Chatelaine. The town that never changes. Harv's New BBQ straight ahead."

Her phone rang, and Carrie answered with a smile. "Hey, Kelsey." Her best friend from Albuquerque called her almost every day to check on her. Actually, several of her friends did, stepping in to be her family when her grandparents who raised her had died. She didn't know what she'd do without them, especially now that Randi was gone, too.

"Whatcha up to?" Kelsey asked.

"We're taking a walk through the one-horse town," she answered with a laugh.

"Air is good," Kelsey said. "What about people?"

Carrie shrugged. "Haven't seen a lot of them, but then again, I haven't really gone searching for them, either."

Her friend's tone turned serious. "Don't cut yourself off from everyone, Car. You need people."

"Which is why I've got you, and Emma and Olivia."

The four of them had been a group all throughout school. Even now, they remained close.

"Yes, you'll always have us," Kelsey said. "But you're not in Albuquerque any longer. You need to make friends in Texas, too."

She sighed. "I don't know, Kels. I'm probably not staying here much longer. Only as long as it takes to get Randi and Isaac's estate settled and Aviva's adoption finalized."

"You never know," Kelsey said. "Just promise me you'll try."

"Okay, I will."

Carrie hung up the phone and thought about this town Randi and Isaac had lived in. Growing up outside Albuquerque, Carrie had thought her hometown was small, but it was a thriving metropolis compared to Chatelaine. It also had a thriving Jewish community of which she'd been a part. Still, this place had charm. As much as thoughts of the funeral pained her, Carrie had been touched by the presence of what seemed like the entire town at the service and shiva afterward. Although her brother-in-law wasn't observant and the funeral itself had been nondenominational, his parents had thought having mourners gather after the service was a lovely idea, and the shiva had enabled Carrie to grieve with her Jewish faith in mind. And the townsfolk had agreed.

As she walked down the street, she chatted to Aviva, pointing out the dogs on leashes, the birds in the sky and the different cowboy hats they saw.

They paused outside the local bookstore. A weathered sign with Remi's Reads in robin's-egg blue lettering welcomed them. A woman with long sleek brown hair who appeared close to Carrie's age looked up from where she was fluffing pillows on the benches outside. She stood by the doorway, her porcelain skin flushed, and she waved them inside.

"Hey, y'all, come on in." The woman bent down and smiled at Aviva. "Aren't you just the cutest little thing." Rising, she held out her hand to Carrie, sorrow darkening her long-lashed deep brown eyes almost to black. "I'm Remi. I'm so sorry for your loss. Your sister used to come in and browse all the time. She loved mysteries and playing with Aviva in our children's section." Remi blinked before continuing. "She was a doll. Such a tragedy."

"Thank you. She talked about how much she loved your bookstore." Carrie's eyes filled, and she forced her tears away. Although everyone seemed to know everyone else in this town, she didn't, and she felt weird sharing her sorrow with strangers, no matter how kindhearted they might be.

"How are you adjusting to living here and taking care of your sweet niece?"

Carrie shrugged. Ideally, she wanted to return to Albuquerque in the near future, but she wasn't going to confess that here. "She's wonderful, and I love her to pieces. I haven't figured out what I'm going to do yet, or how, though."

Remi nodded. "You've got time. Don't rush anything."

Her neck tightened. *Time.* Her sister and brother-in-law were supposed to have time, too. She shook her head, trying not to let the grief overwhelm her.

"If you'd like to browse, we've got lots of new releases over here," she said, pointing to a tall, labeled bookcase. "Unless you're going somewhere special?"

Carrie didn't know if Remi knew she needed to change the subject or was just naturally curious. Part of her was grateful for the segue, another part of her was hesitant to answer in the face of such blatant curiosity. She tried to squelch that part.

"We're just getting some fresh air."

"It's a shame you weren't here a half hour ago. Arlo Fortune was in. Poor man looked so sad. It must be terrible for him to lose his father and best friend, one right after the other. I feel so bad for him." She brightened when Aviva started bouncing in her stroller. "I'll bet he'd have loved to see Aviva."

Everyone in Chatelaine and the surrounding area knew the Fortune name. Even Carrie, who only came by to visit her sister, recognized it. She knew from chatting with Randi that Arlo had been a good friend of her brother-in-law's. She vaguely remembered him from the crush of people at the funeral. Tall, longish sandy hair, sorrowful green eyes.

"Another time," she said.

Remi nodded. "Don't hesitate to stop by if you need anything or just want some company."

Carrie thanked her before waving goodbye and exiting the store. There were so many things she needed; it was overwhelming. And as nice as it was to have people offer to help her, the one person she relied on for help—her sister—was gone. Without her, Carrie didn't know what to do.

Arlo Fortune leaned back in his brown calf-leather desk chair and rubbed his eyes. He'd stared at the computer screen, going over the Fortune Family Ranch's expenses for what seemed like hours. His eyes were gritty, and his head ached.

The good news was that Dahlia's plans for the new

sheep were on track. With the first shearing of the herd taking place in the spring, she'd be able to sell the wool in bulk as well as spin it into yarn to sell. Arlo was comfortable telling Nash, his brother and ranch foreman, to expect a profit in the next two to three months. His brother would be happy.

Arlo should be as well, but his heart wasn't invested in the ranch at the moment. Even though it should be. When he'd first found out his mom had bought the ranch from an older couple who'd retired to Arizona, he'd been thrilled to put his skills to work in building the spread into a successful venture. The fact that it would have ticked off his dad, who expected his kids to go into business like him, was an added bonus. But his heart was aching—in anger at his late father and in sorrow for his best friend. The anger was nothing new. He'd been pissed at his dad for what seemed his entire life. Casper Windham was a ruthless bastard who put business before his family. His mom might have accepted it, but he never would. To think his father might have betrayed his family, though? And to be unable to confront him about it? He fumed.

Usually, he'd talk to his best friend, Isaac. But the last time they'd talked, they'd argued over his father's potential betrayal. And then Isaac had died. He closed his eyes. Even after a month, it still hurt. Seemed like all his relationships were up in the air, unable to be resolved. If only he could let them go.

Shoot, it had been a month, and he hadn't checked on Aviva, his best friend's daughter, or Carrie, the sister-in-law who was now her guardian. The last time he'd seen either of them had been at the shiva. He'd been filled with sorrow and good intentions, but while the grief lasted, the good intentions had disappeared into thin air.

With a sigh, he pushed away from the desk and walked outside. Taking a walk into town earlier and stopping at Remi's Reads hadn't helped him. Maybe talking to the animals might.

Midday, the sun was high overhead, and although it was only in the midfifties, he was comfortable in his shirt-sleeves. He left the main building where his office was and walked along the dirt path from the cream-stucco office building to one of the red barns. On a sunny day like this, he'd usually spend time admiring the beauty of the ranch, but today, he just didn't care. With the doors wide open on either end, a refreshing breeze aired it out. The weak sunlight highlighted dust motes and pieces of hay floating in the air. The cattle in their stalls huffed and stomped, knocking their feed trays.

He paused in the doorway and inhaled the scent of hay and sawdust, wood and manure. Although he never imagined himself as a rancher, there was something about being in the barn that centered him.

If his father could see him now.

The mood that was lifting now soured. Casper had hated everything about ranching. It was "beneath him," and he'd thought Arlo was wasting his time. He never would have understood this feeling. Shaking his shoulders as if by doing so he could rid himself of the uncomfortable memories, he strode the length of the barn, checking in on the cattle inside, stopping to pet a nose or to exchange a word or two with one of the ranch hands.

"Hey, Arlo," Heath Blackwood, his soon to be brother-in-law, called out. His sister Jade was head over heels in love with him, and Arlo couldn't be happier for the newly engaged couple. Her happiness was the one thing capable of piercing his overwhelming sadness. The tall man stepped into the main corridor of the barn, the sun glinting off his sandy hair. "How's your drone analysis going? Did you get a chance to look into the supporting documents I gave you?"

Arlo nodded. "I'm really impressed with how AI technology can help kill weeds without pesticides."

The other man's blue eyes gleamed. "Yeah, me, too. I think it might give the industry a profitable way to go green."

Arlo leaned against one of the stall doors, absently petting the nose of one of the many horses they kept. "I've started to read up on it, and I love the idea of getting rid of pesticides," he said. "I'm just not sure how it helps ranchers like us. If we were farming crops, I'd be fully on board. Any chance you can get me more information on how it applies to us?"

Heath nodded. "I get it. I was skeptical, too, at first. I'll send what I have over to you today. I want to make sure we have this handled before Christmas. I don't want to mess up your holiday plans."

Arlo scoffed. "No worries. I'm not doing anything for Christmas this year, so nothing you do will mess me up."

"Not celebrating Christmas?" Heath's eyes widened. "Why not?"

Why the heck did he open his mouth? He could have just volunteered to get the work done in plenty of time and not brought up the holiday. Now, not only did he have to answer the man, but the entire family would probably hear about it and make his next month a living hell.

"Don't mind me, Heath. I'm just grumpy today."

His sister's fiancé stared at him long and hard. "You sure that's all it is?" he asked.

Arlo nodded. "Trust me. And don't worry, we'll get everything finished before Christmas."

He wasn't fooled into thinking the matter was settled, but Heath let him off with a nod, and Arlo exited the barn before the man had second thoughts. He walked along the drive, trying to air out his melancholy. In the distance, Christmas lights decorated the barbed wire fencing. Up against one side of the barn, an old tractor tire was painted green, and someone had tied a huge bright red bow on it. And out by the petting zoo on the other side of the barns, bales of hay were painted white, piled on top of each other, and decorated to look like snow men.

His family thought the decorations made the ranch look festive.

As for him? Well, he thought it looked like a mischievous elf had thrown up Christmas dust everywhere.

With a growl, he stalked back to his office, shut his blinds and stared defiantly at his computer. He was aware of his mood but didn't care. Isaac used to be able to tease him out of it, but his best friend wasn't here anymore. He didn't care who disagreed with him. He wasn't celebrating the holiday this year.

With Aviva finally down for her nap, Carrie stood outside Isaac's home office, staring at the closed door. It was time to tackle the beast, but she'd been putting it off for way too long. Even going through her sister's closet had been preferable to entering Isaac's office. She'd sorted Randi's clothing, given most of it away, but kept a few pieces that held memories of the time she'd spent with her sister. She'd also kept a few maternity pieces to show Aviva when she was older, in case she wanted them as mementos of her mom, in addition to a few random scarves and shoes for the little girl to play dress-up. Although the items were personal, somehow she was able to convince herself she was doing a mitzvah by donating the clothes her sister would no longer wear, and therefore, even though she'd cried, she'd also laughed, remembering the good times they'd had together.

But Isaac's office? Ugh.

The only reason she had to go in there was his death. She'd yet to decide whether to sell the house or make it her own, but she couldn't do either if she didn't clean it out. Time was passing, though, and Aviva would be waking from her nap soon, so no matter how much she wanted to avoid the chore, she had to do it. Better to tackle the job on her terms.

Taking a deep breath, she opened the door to his home office. The drapes were closed, leaving the room in darkness, and a month of being shut up tight left it with a stuffy, musty smell. She opened the navy drapes, letting the winter light into the room. She wanted to open a window, but the chill outside made her pause. Dust motes floated in the light. A hint of Isaac's aftershave permeated the room.

She surveyed the space, deciding to tackle first what she dreaded most—his desk. The large oak piece of furniture took up a good chunk of one wall. A brown leather chair still held the imprint of his body. It didn't feel right to sit in it, but then again, it felt wrong to be in here in the first place. With a sigh, she sat on the edge of the chair, whispered an "I'm sorry" to Isaac's spirit and examined the surface of the desk.

A leather inbox sat in the upper right corner, filled with mail. She took the papers and sorted through them, making notes to check bank accounts and forward necessary pieces to his business partners.

She took the photo of Aviva—a smiling close-up showing two teeth and a little drool—and put it in the keeper pile. She pictured it in her bedroom on her dresser. The other photos, a framed copy of their wedding photo and a candid of Randi at a barbecue, made her tear up. She'd display them somewhere so Aviva could see them. She didn't want the child to forget her parents.

Finally, it was time to look inside the drawers. Invading Isaac's privacy still bothered her. She'd never been involved in his business, didn't know what he did other than financial consulting. But what if she discovered something she shouldn't?

She loved her brother-in-law, but everyone had bits of themselves they kept hidden from the rest of the world. What if he had a secret that changed how she thought about him? She'd never be able to ask him to explain what she found and would have to live with her interpretation of the news. Carrie bit her lip. The idea of asking someone else to go through his things flitted through her brain, but she tossed it aside. His colleagues had gone through his office at work already. It was her job to go through his private desk, no matter how distasteful the idea might be.

She took a deep breath before she opened the front drawer of his desk. On the left was his tablet. She smiled. Isaac had never been without it for long, constantly using it to jot down ideas for whatever project he was currently

working on. It had been a bone of contention between
Randi and him, although she'd always complained in a
loving way about how he could never escape from his job.
When Aviva was born, he'd used it as a camera as well.
After trying a few password ideas, Aviva's birthday finally
unlocked the tablet. She nodded as she scrolled through the
apps and photos. Placing it on the desk in her keeper pile,
she continued to sort through the drawer, digging through
office supplies until she came to a yellow legal pad. Even
a techie like Isaac had to go old-school once in a while.

The first page was a handwritten letter to Arlo.

Dear Arlo,

The first few lines were crossed out, and she couldn't
make out the words, but then,

*I want to set things right between us. Our friend-
ship means more to me than any argument. I never
should have given—*

The letter stopped there.
Frowning, Carrie turned the page.

Dear Arlo,

We never should have fought over—the lines were
crossed out.

The name, Arlo, was uncommon enough. Did he mean
Arlo Fortune? She'd learned that Fortune was a big name
in Chatelaine, and Arlo had paid a shiva call. She vaguely
recalled him at the funeral, too, although that day had
been a blur.

Her throat thickened. Had Isaac died with Arlo angry at him? She leaned back in her brother-in-law's desk chair. Isaac had always grabbed hold of what he wanted. He was loyal and defended those he loved. She couldn't imagine his letting an argument go without resolving it, especially with a friend. Carrie shook her head, saddened at the unfinished business, then moved the pad to the side and found a white envelope peeking out from the bottom of the drawer. The envelope was addressed to Arlo Fortune. There was no address given, but she recognized Isaac's handwriting. How many times had she seen it on notes written to her sister or birthday cards he'd sent to her? She traced the writing with her finger, missing the kind man who'd never failed to make her laugh. She flipped the envelope over, but it was sealed.

Her eyes welled with tears. Was this the letter he'd been writing but never sent? Was he waiting for the right time or having second thoughts? He'd died before he could send it. Her shoulders shook with silent grief as she cried about all the opportunities Isaac and Randi missed.

Holding the letter in her hand, she wondered what argument could separate good friends. Randi hadn't mentioned anything to her, even though they had spoken daily. Her sister was her best friend, and it killed her they could no longer talk to each other. Her sympathy for Arlo swelled.

She had no idea what they'd argued about, but she had to deliver the letter to him. Clearly, Isaac had been trying to patch things up between them. Maybe he'd tried unsuccessfully in person, and this letter was his last resort. Or perhaps he was trying to start the conversation with him by writing him a letter, intending to talk face-to-face later. He'd died before any of those events could happen.

She owed it to Arlo to give him the letter in person. Right away.

Still uncomfortable using Isaac's computer, she punched in Aviva's birthday again, and when it succeeded, she shook her head at his poor computer security and opened her laptop to search for Arlo's address. Randi had told her the Fortunes bought a huge ranch on the far side of Lake Chatelaine last summer. It had been the talk of the town, and she remembered her sister's conversations about it.

"Carrie, you wouldn't believe the opulence," Randi had said one afternoon while they were chatting. "All the Fortunes live right on the lake in these big fancy cabins. Ha, not that they're the kind of cabins you or I would think of, though."

Carrie had pulled away from an article she was writing about energy drinks and rubbed her eyes. Staring at a laptop all day killed her eyes, and she'd been thrilled to take a break and chat with her sister.

"Really? Do you ever see them in town? What's the family like?"

"I only know one of them, Arlo Fortune. He's Isaac's best friend and is a really nice guy. Smart, too. They call him the 'ranch whisperer.'"

"Why? Does he whisper to cows or something? That seems kind of strange."

Randi had laughed. "No, but he takes failing ranches and turns them around. Even the most hopeless ones. And Aviva loves him."

What would Randi think of her bringing the letter to Arlo? Carrie smiled through her tears. She'd probably insist on going just so she could take a look at the wealthy area.

Carrie paused. Showing up unannounced was odd.

Maybe she should check to see if she could find a phone number for him, to let him know what she found and to find out if he wanted her to give him the letter. He hardly knew her, even if she was Aviva's aunt. Some people didn't like surprises.

Just then, the monitor squawked to life with Aviva's voice.

She walked into the toddler's yellow and white nursery. Ducks painted on the border of the walls right below the ceiling had always made her smile. Aviva sat up in her white toddler bed with the guard rails and gave her aunt a toothy grin. Her blond curls were mussed from sleeping and tumbled all over her head.

"Hello, muffin," Carrie said, joy shooting through her body. Somehow, the little girl always made her smile.

"Wo. Up. Up now."

Carrie chuckled. "Yes, you want to get up now. I see that."

She lowered the guardrail and let Aviva climb out of her bed. Knowing the routine, the toddler wobbled to the changing table and grabbed a diaper, the tush of her pants sagging.

"Change now, pwese."

Some toddlers' favorite word was *no*. Aviva's was *now*. At least she said please.

"Yes, ma'am."

Aviva giggled her way through the change and then brought her stuffed elephant with her downstairs with Carrie.

Carrie fixed her a snack of bananas and cheese cubes and sat her in her booster seat at the kitchen table. She brought her milk in her blue sippy cup and, once the child was settled, opened her laptop in the seat next to her.

She entered Arlo Fortune's name in the search bar, hoping to find a phone number, but nothing came up other than his address. Frowning, she tried again, without any luck.

With one eye on Aviva, she scanned the room. Where would Randi and Isaac keep Arlo's phone number? She didn't doubt they'd had it, but they'd probably kept it in their phones, and unfortunately, those had been destroyed in the accident.

She sighed.

Aviva leaned over and patted Carrie's shoulder.

"Iss okay," she said in her little voice. "Iss okay."

Carrie kissed Aviva's head. "I should be saying that to you, little one."

Aviva scrunched her face. "I big girl."

Laughing, Carrie responded, "Yes, you are." She pretended to try to lift Aviva up and groaned. "Oh, my goodness, you *are* big!"

Peals of laughter echoed in the kitchen, filling Carrie's heart with joy. Cleaned off and out of her booster seat, Aviva raised her arms over her head.

"Big, big, big," she chanted as she marched around the room.

"Well, then, it's time to take this big girl on a ride."

"Wide?" Aviva asked.

Carrie nodded. "Ride." If she couldn't call Arlo, then she was going to have to hand deliver the letter. She just hoped he wouldn't mind a surprise visitor.

Chapter Two

Arlo was sitting at his desk, buried in strategic plans for the ranch, when Maria, the part-time receptionist, knocked on his office door.

"Yeah," he said, his eyes glued to his computer. He had one more piece of information to work out before he could sign off on the plans, and he hated to break his concentration.

"Arlo, you have a visitor," Maria said.

He looked up, and his eyes widened at the sight of Carrie. He rose when he saw Aviva in her arms.

"Thanks, Maria. Carrie, Aviva, this is a nice surprise." He ushered them into his small office and looked for a place for them to sit. The ranch offices were located in a 1950s ranch-style home, where the original owners had lived before they'd expanded. When the Fortunes had taken over the property, they'd renovated the house into workspaces, and Arlo's office was in the former utility room. Usually, it suited his needs fine. He preferred working in his house on the lake, but when he needed to interact with his sisters and brothers, he worked here.

But his office wasn't set up for visitors. The room was small, with a simple metal desk and ergonomic chair. The two chairs on the other side of his desk were filled with paperwork that he hadn't yet gotten around to filing. That was to be his project during the holidays, when the rest of his family were off celebrating.

He swept one chair clean, piling the papers and folders on the floor in the corner.

"Here, sit down," he said.

Carrie looked amused. "I didn't think you'd recognize me," she said.

"I remember you from the funeral and shiva."

A frown flashed across her face, disappearing as quickly as it appeared. She looked around the office.

"You have an interesting filing method," she murmured.

He huffed. "It's not my strong suit."

He stared at the pretty woman seated across from him. The last time he'd seen her she was deep in mourning, with sadness etched into her face, her eyes deep with misery.

Now, well, he suspected she was still in mourning, but she hid it better. Carrie's dark brown hair was pulled back into a ponytail, with a few strands escaping around her oval face. Her hands were graceful, her nails polished pale pink, and she held Aviva's chubby hands in hers.

Aviva.

He smiled at the rosy-cheeked toddler, seeing his best friend in the shape of her mouth and the dimple in her chin.

"What can I do for you?"

Discomfort crossed Carrie's face. She began to unzip Aviva's jacket, and Arlo wasn't sure if the task was for the child's benefit or to give her something to do.

"I was going through Isaac's desk and came across these items. I thought you'd want them."

She handed him a yellow legal pad and a sealed envelope. He'd recognize that handwriting anywhere.

His chest tightened.

Grief and regret mingled and caused him to lash out. "What are you doing with this? Did you read it?"

Aviva hid her head in Carrie's shoulder. Guilt flooded through him.

"I read the legal pad because it was out in the open, and I was trying to figure out what it was," she said matter-of-factly. "And like I said, I was going through his desk at home."

He and Isaac had been best friends as children. He should have figured there might be things for him in Isaac's possessions. But the thought of this woman going through them felt like a violation of privacy.

He didn't want things. He wanted his friend.

"What gave you the right to read any of it?" He knew he shouldn't lash out at her, but he couldn't help it.

Carrie's eyes widened. She straightened, tightening her hold on Aviva. "He was my family."

Arlo paused to gather his thoughts and his breath. He looked at the envelope. Still sealed. Rationality returned. She wasn't prying; she was going through the horrible chore of sifting through her sister and brother-in-law's things.

The rest of his anger fizzled, like a soda pop going flat.

"I'm sorry," he said. "I shouldn't have jumped on you like that. I was wrong."

"You're in mourning, too," Carrie replied, her voice low. She rubbed Aviva's back, the repetitive motion soothing.

For a moment, the thought of her soothing *him* flashed through his mind, gone as quickly as it came.

"Isaac was my friend, but he was your family. I appreciate your generosity."

She nodded as he swirled his hand over the handwriting on the legal pad.

Dear Arlo,

I want to set things right between us. Our friend-ship means more to me than any argument. I never should have given—

He stared at the words as they blurred before his eyes. Isaac had wanted to apologize. Waves of grief overcame him. What a waste. Instead of spending weeks angry at each other, they could have worked out their differences and had extra time. He'd give anything for even an hour or two at this point, and to think he could have had an entire month.

A tap on his knee brought him back to the present. Aviva was touching his leg and holding out her arms to him. He forced a smile, leaning down to pick her up. As he gave her a hug, her sweet toddler smell washed away some of his sadness.

"Hello, pretty girl. I haven't seen you in a while. I'm sorry."

"Sowwy."

"That's right, I'm sorry."

He glanced at Carrie. Her wariness unsettled him, but then, with how angry he was, he shouldn't be surprised about her nerves around him.

Aviva lifted her arms up, and he laughed. Rising out of his chair, he lifted her up over his head and placed her on his shoulders. She squealed.

Carrie rose, looking like she wanted to pull Aviva off him, but he adjusted the child and held on to her feet.

His smooth, confident movements must have put her at ease because she sat down again.

"What animal should I be today?" he asked Aviva. It

was their favorite game to play together, and even though it had been a while since he'd last seen her, and longer still since they'd played this game, she remembered.

"Chicken!" she yelled. "Cwuck, cwuck!"

His office was small, and with Carrie sitting across from his desk it felt even smaller. But he squatted and shuffled around in a circle, yelling, "Cluck, cluck." The child's peals of laughter soothed his soul, and even made Carrie smile.

Or maybe she was smiling at his ridiculous actions.

He certainly didn't look like a chicken, although he did feel like one. His mood darkened, but he tried to hide it from Aviva. He hadn't liked what her father had said, and instead of listening to him or considering his suggestion, he'd gotten angry and walked away. And then, instead of being a mature adult and apologizing, he'd done nothing.

It was his fault they hadn't made peace with each other before Isaac died, and all because he was a coward. Suddenly, the game wasn't fun anymore.

Carrie watched in equal parts fascination, discomfort and humor as this man she barely knew clucked like a chicken, waddling around in circles in this small, barely-big-enough-for-an-office space. His tall, muscular frame made his ridiculous movements look easy. His green eyes crinkled when he smiled, and his cheeks had sexy dimples. *Sexy?* She shook her head in equal parts confusion and denial.

Nothing had gone the way she'd expected today. The lack of control made her antsy.

Arlo knew who she was even before she introduced herself, which was odd since they barely knew each other. Back home in Albuquerque, that didn't happen, but she was quickly learning Chatelaine, Texas, was a far cry from New Mexico.

Even so, who would have thought a Fortune would know her? Yet he had and didn't think it was strange she was stopping by unannounced.

What kind of a wealthy investor had a tiny office barely big enough for antics he apparently was used to performing? Wouldn't you think he'd have kept that in mind when he'd set up his office in the first place? Or hadn't he planned to cluck like a chicken at work? Maybe he saved that behavior for his off hours. It was a good thing Aviva hadn't asked for a giraffe.

Her niece was so at ease with him, a small sliver of jealousy sliced through her. And then she took herself to task. She wasn't about to be jealous of Aviva's love of this man. There were few enough of those in the two-year-old's life, and she wasn't about to take this away from her. Her heart seized. What would happen if she moved back to Albuquerque with Aviva? One of the best reasons to do so was to give her sister's child a bigger Jewish community. But would Aviva form such a connection with other men she met there, ones who were complete strangers?

With a mental shake, she looked on in amusement as Arlo continued to cluck and waddle in circles. She wasn't sure what to do. Aviva's laughter was contagious, and a part of her wanted to participate, to do something to cause the tyke to laugh with her, too. But she'd never been one to let down her guard enough in front of strangers, and he *was* kind of a stranger to her.

As she stood there watching the two of them play together, a shadow crossed Arlo's face. His step hitched, but he recovered before she had a chance to say anything, or even wonder if she should say something to him. A couple minutes of play later, he swung Aviva off his shoulders.

"Whew, this chicken is tired!"

Setting Aviva on the floor gently, he made sure the toddler had her balance before he looked over at Carrie.

"You must think I'm crazy," he said.

"You mean like a chicken without his head?"

He laughed, and Carrie admired this handsome man who wasn't too full of himself to play with a child and act the fool.

"No," she added. "I don't think you're crazy. I'm glad Aviva has someone in her life like you." She rummaged in her bag for a container of Goldfish, opened the top and handed it to the little girl.

"Here you go, sweetie."

"Tank you," she said.

"You're welcome." She didn't know a lot about raising a toddler, but she'd figured out that if she encouraged and modeled manners, they'd continue.

"You're very good with her," Arlo said as he watched the child munch the cheesy crackers.

"You are, too."

His green eyes pierced hers, filled with sorrow. "I'm very sorry for your loss," he said, his deep voice scratchy. He cleared it, an endearing action that filled her with sympathy. She'd received a lot of consolations during this past month, but Arlo's felt different. Like he was almost as affected as she was.

Like he understood.

Squatting next to her niece to make sure she didn't make a mess of the small office, she looked up at him.

"Thank you. I'm sorry for your loss, too. It's hard to lose a friend."

He nodded. "Especially when we—"

At her quizzical look, he swallowed before continuing. "We fought before his death and never made peace. He'll never know how sorry I am, or how much his friendship meant to me."

Carrie's heart melted, even as her throat thickened with tears she couldn't allow herself to shed. Not here, and not in front of Aviva. The girl had been around way too much sadness in her short life.

She cleared her throat and tipped her chin at the letter in Arlo's hand. The one she hadn't opened.

Neither had he.

"Maybe reading the letter will help."

He stared at it, moving it from hand to hand, turning it over and over, like Torah students searching for hidden meanings.

Without overthinking, she reached for his hand and squeezed it. Not for any other reason but to share some sympathy. She didn't expect to notice how strong his hand was, how large, how warm the skin.

She didn't expect him to squeeze back.

Arlo still held the letter in his hand after Carrie and Aviva left his office. He'd walked them to the door and watched them leave, the attractive woman and the tiny child. With their departure, his office felt small and airless. All the joy disappeared with them. He sighed, the letter weighing on him more than its actual few ounces.

He stared at it. What if reading it made him feel worse?

Shaking himself off, he silently rebuked the thoughts

crowding his mind, almost hearing his father's voice scoffing in the background.

You'll never know if you don't open it. And maybe it will actually make you feel better.

Closing his door for privacy, he sat behind his desk, grabbed a gold letter opener with an engraved *W* on the handle—one of the things he'd taken from his father's personal belongings—and slit open the seal.

He clenched his teeth and began to read:

Dear Arlo,

Your friendship means a lot to me. I had no right to try to make you look at the situation with your dad and the misdelivered toys differently. Yeah, you're right, I wanted that to be about something else. But you know I had issues with my own father, and making peace with him before he passed changed me for the good to the point that I soon met the woman I would marry. I'm a husband and father because I let my own past go. I just want the same for you. But I'm sorry for trying to bulldoze you about it. Let's put it aside.

—Isaac

He dropped his head onto his desk. His breath whooshed out of him like a deflating balloon. Isaac had apologized to him. Although he'd never be able to tell his best friend he forgave him, just knowing Isaac's thoughts prior to his death was a huge relief. Memories of the day of their fight swirled in his brain, but this time, others drove them away. Their first day of rodeo camp, when Arlo had reassured Isaac that the horses were friendly; s'mores-eating contests…and getting sick afterward; the cowboy song they'd created and sung together. There were also more adult memories—visiting each other over college breaks; conversations about investing strategies; Isaac's excitement at finding "the perfect place to live near camp," and then his surprise and pleasure when Arlo and his family moved here.

So many wonderful times together. He wished there could be more.

He remembered his friend's nuptials. It had been the first time he'd attended a Jewish wedding, and he'd been fascinated by the customs—stepping on a glass, the bride circling the groom, the wedding canopy. Isaac and Randi had looked joyous. He remembered being pleased for them, but there were also shards of jealousy, wondering if he'd ever find someone who made him as happy as they made each other feel.

He still wondered that sometimes.

Sighing, he raised his head and flattened the letter on the desk. Thanks to his friend's words, he could look back at their relationship with less pain than he'd felt in more than a month.

If he couldn't have settled things between Isaac and himself before the accident, at least he knew his friend had forgiven him. It wasn't perfect, but it was much better than before.

When Isaac and Randi had moved to Chatelaine, they'd raved about small-town life. When Randi had gotten pregnant, Isaac had talked to Arlo about the prospect of teaching his child how to ride a horse.

Well, Isaac was gone now, but *he* was here. Maybe he could talk to Carrie about getting Aviva horseback riding lessons someday. Heck, he had an entire ranch filled with his siblings who worked on it. His sister Dahlia was a sheep farmer. Jade led children's workshops and ran a petting zoo. Even his brother Ridge was a cowboy. One of them could come up with something. Plus, he needed to thank Carrie for giving him the letter.

Chapter Three

Arlo drove into town, past GreatStore, Remi's Reads and the Cowgirl Café. They were decorated for Christmas, with lights strung around their windows. A sign in the window of GreatStore advertised the yearly Christmas cookie contest to be held at the local church. Everywhere he looked, there were signs of the holiday. He turned off the main road onto Carrie's street. As it happened every time he pulled into the driveway, his mind couldn't grasp that Isaac and Randi were gone. He expected them to open the door and give him a hug and a clap on the back as they always had. But when he exited his truck, loped up the front steps and rang the doorbell, they didn't answer.

Carrie did.

"Arlo," she said, surprise showing on her face. "Come in." She opened the door wide, and he stepped into the familiar-but-not front hallway, removing his cowboy hat and placing it on the hall coat rack, as usual. Carrie had left the rack but changed the hallway, adding photos of her sister and brother-in-law on the entryway table. The sight of them gave him both pleasure and pain. He hadn't fully thought this through.

To his right, in the living room, Aviva sat on the floor playing with toys.

"I hope I'm not disturbing you," he said, rocking back and forth in his boots.

Carrie had her dark hair tied back in a loose ponytail. Wisps on either side of her face had escaped. She wore tight-fitting jeans that showed off her long legs, and a soft-looking pink sweater that made her cheeks glow.

"Not at all." She turned to her niece. "We love company, right?"

Aviva put her hands on the floor and stood up, then ran over to Arlo and grabbed his leg.

Grinning, he swung her up in the air. "Hello, munchkin!"

She squeezed his neck, and he inhaled her little-girl smell. The more he saw her, the greater the pull he felt for her. She was the living, breathing embodiment of her parents.

"Would you like to come in?" Carrie asked. Her voice brought him back into the moment.

He looked at her, and he thought he saw understanding flash across her face, but it was gone before he could be sure.

Nodding, he followed her into the living room. She motioned to the deep gray suede couch, and he sat. Aviva wiggled out of his grasp and returned to her toys on the gray-and-green-striped rug. He scanned the room. Once again, there were photos of Isaac, Randi and Aviva everywhere.

"I don't want Aviva to forget them," Carrie said.

"So, you're going to stay?"

"For now."

The answer pleased him. "I'm happy to hear that. It gives me more time to spend with Aviva." Being separated from the child had been especially hard during his estrangement from Isaac, and he was looking forward to making up for lost time.

Turning his thoughts from Aviva to her aunt, he glanced at Carrie sitting on the corner of the couch. She was quieter than most women he knew. On the ranch, his sisters were constantly in motion, Dahlia working with her sheep and expanding the dairy farm, Sabrina crunching the numbers and Jade leading children's workshops. But Carrie was still. At least, her *body* was. He'd bet there was a lot going on in her brain. There was something about the way she observed everything that spoke to him.

"I wanted to thank you for bringing me the letter and the legal pad," he said, when the silence had stretched a moment too long. "They were really helpful."

Her expression softened. "I'm so glad. I don't know what the letter said, but based on what I saw written on the legal pad, well, I hope you were able to get some closure."

He ran a hand over the top of his head. "Closure. That's a tough word. I don't know if that's possible, but after reading the letter, I feel better knowing Isaac forgives me."

His stomach clenched. He hadn't meant to blurt that out.

"How are you doing?" he asked. It was a long overdue question.

She redirected her gaze to Aviva, who continued to play with her toys. "I don't know," she admitted. "I love Aviva more than anything in the world. I thought I was coming here to babysit for a week. Next thing I know, I've lost my sister and brother-in-law, I'm living in a small ranching town, and I'm responsible for raising her and for teaching her all about her religion. It's such a huge change. I haven't had a moment to breathe, let alone think about how I'm doing."

Gosh, he should have checked in on her sooner. Of course, she was overwhelmed. Meanwhile, he'd been sitting with his head up his butt like a rodeo clown.

"I remember Randi being so excited you were coming. And Isaac, who had been nervous about leaving Aviva for a week, relaxed as soon as Randi told him you'd be babysitting." He turned to look at Carrie. "They had a lot of faith in you."

Her dark eyes welled with tears. "Thank you. That's nice to know."

"Tell me about Randi," he said quietly. "What was she like as a big sister?"

"Bossy," Carrie answered with a laugh. "No, I guess that's not true. She always looked out for me when we were growing up. It used to annoy me at times, but then when she had Aviva, I realized she was just a mothering type. It wasn't in her nature to let those she cared about suffer, so she was always trying to help me."

Arlo nodded. "Yeah, I understand that. I have five other siblings, and one of them was always trying to boss someone around. Usually me, since everyone but Ridge is older than I am."

"How did you and Isaac meet?" she asked. "I remember he was so excited to be moving here near where he went to camp."

"We met at a rodeo camp when we were seven." He chuckled. "We were the unlikeliest rodeo cowboys you'd ever met, at least that first year. We were both small and skinny and hadn't been around horses before."

Carrie laughed, and Arlo warmed to the topic. "Isaac grew up in Dallas and was a total city kid, and I grew up in a small town outside Dallas without any knowledge of horses, either. So, I guess we decided teaming up together was our best course of action."

Nodding, Carrie said, "I'll bet."

"By the end of the summer, we were horse crazy. We kept in touch all during the year, even though my dad thought rodeo horses were beneath me." He swallowed. "As we got older and returned to camp yearly, we started to be known for our skills not just with horses, but activities involved with running the camp. As adults, we turned that knowledge into our businesses."

"Wow, you got all of that experience at a rodeo camp?"

He nodded. "You'd be surprised how well horse skills can translate into other ones."

"How so?" Carrie asked curiously.

Arlo adjusted his body and got comfortable. "Well, I can look at a horse—his movements, his eyes, his breathing— and know how reliable that horse is. That skill translates to people. I can get a good sense how trustworthy a person is based on their body language. And when I'm taking a look at the books on the business side, I use my knowledge of the people—as well as the animals they use—to determine how successful that ranch is going to be."

"That's incredible."

"Not really. You just have to understand a ranch is more than just numbers." He rolled a ball to Aviva, who rolled it back to him. "What about you? What do you do?"

"I'm a writer. I write health and wellness articles for a variety of online sites."

"Really? That's cool. What kinds of articles?"

"A lot of food and nutrition, with some mental health thrown in as well." She looked around before continuing. "I'm actually considering pitching a grief journey series to my editors. Unfortunately, I've learned a lot about that in the past month, and I think my experiences could help others."

"I think that's a great idea," Arlo said thickly. "Maybe it will give you an outlet, help you process everything. I know that's been my struggle."

He paused. Had he really just confessed that to her, almost a complete stranger? He studied her. She wasn't *really* a complete stranger. In some ways, he'd been more open with her than he had been with his siblings. And nothing about her hinted that she'd use anything he said to her advantage. She oozed kindness and compassion.

"It's something that's been tough for me, too. Which is why I want to write about it, even if no one publishes it." She focused on Aviva for a few moments. "Now I just have to find the time to do it, right, cutie?"

"Pay wif bocks?" Aviva asked, holding one up.

As Carrie took it and started to build a tower, Arlo marveled at her strength. She'd lost her sister and brother-in-law, had taken over the care of her niece and had to learn to juggle single-parenthood and a job, as well as her own grief. Yet she wanted to help others, too.

He shook his head as the differences between the two of them stared him in the face. While he'd turned inward, she'd turned outward.

Regret nudged him once again. He really should have offered to help her long before now.

Carrie rose. "I'm getting her a snack. Can I offer you anything to eat or drink?"

"I'll take a Coke if you have it."

She nodded, and he played with Aviva, rebuilding the tower she'd knocked down while Carrie left the room. A few minutes later she returned with a sippy cup and a container of Cheerios for Aviva and two Cokes.

They both drank and watched Aviva for a few moments.

"Are you entering the Christmas cookie contest?" he asked to break the silence. At her quizzical look, he continued. "The town council sponsors it every year. People bake their favorite holiday treats, and the mayor and other town leaders judge. The entry fees go to help the poor. Winners receive a monogrammed apron and a certificate." He grinned. The prize was a little ridiculous, but the cause was good.

Carrie looked thoughtful. "I didn't know about it. I could make *bimuelos*. They're a Hanukkah treat. Do you think that would be okay?"

Arlo nodded. "I'm sure they would. What are they?"

"They're puffed fritters with an orange glaze. It's a Sephardic Jewish tradition for Hanukkah."

"Sephardic?"

Carrie nodded. "Jews who come from Eastern Europe are Ashkenazi, and they have their own foods and traditions that they brought over from Europe. Jews from the Middle East and Spain are Sephardi, and although we have the same religious traditions, our culture reflects where we're from geographically."

"That's fascinating," Arlo said. "I guess now that I think of it, different countries celebrate Christmas differently, too, whether it's food or when we open presents. But I never spent a lot of time considering the differences."

Carrie smiled. "It's so interesting to learn about other cultures and traditions. And sometimes, we even find similarities that we didn't know about."

"Tell me more about Hanukkah," he said. "Those *bimuelos* sound delicious."

"They are," Carrie said. "The holiday, although relatively minor on our calendar, celebrates the miracle of the oil and a military victory from back in ancient times. A small tribe of Jews, the Maccabees, beat a huge army who destroyed their temple. After the battle, the menorah only had enough oil to last one day, but it lasted eight, enough time for the oil to be found and replaced. Since then, we light a special candelabra, called a menorah, one candle each night for eight nights."

"I learned some of that," Arlo said. "I joined Isaac's family once or twice, and they gave me a brief overview. I remember thinking lighting the candles were cool, and you know, eight days of presents had its appeal." He laughed. "Maybe you can teach me more about it."

"Of course." Carrie's face lit up. "There are so many fascinating traditions to being Jewish, and a lot of them involve food."

Arlo rubbed his stomach, making Carrie laugh. "We eat jelly donuts during the holiday because they are fried in oil. When we light the candles, we recite a psalm in honor of the rededication of the Temple. And, since we are Sephardic, coming from the Mediterranean countries rather than the Eastern European ones, we have a big celebration—a *merenda*—on the last night of Hanukkah."

"Looks like Randi chose the perfect person to teach Aviva about her religious culture," he said.

"Thank you," she said. "That's such a nice thing to say. I really want to make sure Aviva doesn't feel alone in her heritage." She released a breath. "And maybe you could share some of your Christmas traditions with me." She gave him a smile that blew him away.

He was so speechless, in fact, that all he could do was nod. When she smiled, it was as if a magnetic field formed around her, drawing him in and making him never want to see that smile dim. Without thinking, he blurted, "My father sent a box of toys to someone right before he died."

"Who'd he send it to?"

"That's just it, I don't know," he muttered. "It was addressed to someone named Stevie Fields, but the address he wrote down doesn't exist. The postman brought it back to the ranch, saying the address was wrong and the mail forwarding listed Windham, our old name, in the system. He was trying to do the right thing and bring it back to us to figure out."

"And did you?"

Arlo shook his head. "Nope." He stared off into the distance. His dad was a mystery, and the box didn't clear anything up. He sighed, focusing on Carrie once again. "I couldn't exactly tell the postman that we'd all moved to Chatelaine to start over, changing our name from Windham to Fortune when my mom found out she was related to that family. Heck, I'm not even sure why I'm telling you, except..." He hesitated. "You're easy to talk to. But the box reminded me of everything I'm trying to forget, and everything I can't fix."

Carrie reached for his hand. "For the past few years, I've been so focused on my writing career, I neglected my family. There were so many times Randi invited me here to spend a weekend to catch up, and I never took her up on it. I always said I was too busy, even though my career was the kind I could do anywhere. It's only now that she's gone that I realize what I missed." She leaned forward. "Have you looked inside the box?"

He nodded, exhaling a deep breath. "It's a box of toys, with a note that said, Dear Stevie, Enjoy these! Casper Windham. My dad was sending toys to some little kid, so that has to mean he had an affair with a woman in Chatelaine and this kid is his second family." He scoffed. "It's just like him to add another mysterious layer when I can't confront him."

"Oh, wow, that must be heartbreaking for you," she said softly. "What do your siblings say? Did they know anything about this?"

He shook his head. "I didn't tell them. They all have their own issues with my dad." He rose and paced the room, hands in his pockets. Confusion swirled through him. "I did tell Isaac, though. That's what we fought about. He was trying to convince me the box of toys could be something completely harmless, but *come on*! This isn't my first rodeo. He was trying to get me to look into it before I jumped to the wrong conclusion, but he didn't know what he was talking about. My dad was a cold, ruthless businessman who always put his company before anyone in his family."

Footsteps behind him warned him Carrie approached a second before she put a comforting hand on his shoulder.

"My dad cheated on my mom when we were young, so I understand the betrayal you're feeling," she confided. "It was the worst time of my life." Her voice grew thoughtful. "We lived outside Albuquerque at the time, and it seemed like everyone knew what happened. They either gave me and my sister pitying looks or whispered behind my mom's back. I was so glad when we moved to Albuquerque proper so I could start over."

Arlo's chest tightened at the image of the childhood Carrie painted. He'd had his family to rely on when his world fell apart, even if he hadn't been the most gracious about accepting their help. In the back of his mind, though, he knew with bone-deep certainty that his siblings and his mom would do anything for him, just as he would for them. Looking back at his upbringing, he realized his mom had always shielded him and his siblings from his dad's life choices. Wendy had supported him and kept him from knowing what other people said, if they'd said anything at all. He still didn't know.

His heart ached knowing Carrie hadn't had that same protection as a young child.

He didn't understand why fathers would put their children through this. Weren't they supposed to love and nurture them? What was wrong with some men? He looked at Aviva. If he were a dad, he'd do everything possible not to hurt his children.

"I just don't get it," he gritted out.

Carrie turned, and he realized he'd spoken out loud. "What don't you get?" she asked.

Once again, whether it was her sympathetic expression or her similar experience, he felt the need to bare his soul.

"I don't get why some men are such jerks when it comes to their families." His fisted his hands at his sides. "And I'll never know why my dad did what he did. Isaac was right, the *not knowing* is killing me. He kept pushing me to look into it, as if finding out whether my dad had an affair or an illegitimate child is going to make a difference."

He heaved himself off the sofa and paced the room. "Isaac just wouldn't let it go. He kept insisting I look up Stevie Fields and that his own good life was testament to the idea that the truth sets you free." He scoffed. "I stalked off and now he's dead." He whispered the last part, his throat aching.

Sniffling made him look back at Carrie. Her eyes were filled with tears, and guilt pierced him. *Great, she's in mourning, and I'm making her cry.*

He'd leave, but it would be even worse to abandon her while she was upset.

"I don't want to butt in, or make you feel worse, but maybe Isaac was right," she said, wiping her eyes. "At least if you know the truth, you'll be able to feel the proper emotions. Look at Isaac. He was adopted, but his adoptive parents kept that a secret from him until he was much older. Not knowing his true past made it hard for him to trust anyone. He was angry at his parents, especially his dad, who had insisted on the secrecy, but they finally talked it all out." She paused for a beat before continuing. "Knowing his background didn't make up for everything, but it helped him realize there wasn't anything wrong with him, and once he learned that information, he and Randi were able to make a wonderful life together."

She turned toward him again when he sat on the sofa. There was something about her voice that calmed him. "If nothing else, it will help you know what to do with those toys," she said.

He groaned. "You're right. And so was Isaac." He ground out those last words, his throat feeling like sandpaper over the admission.

He needed a break. Looking around the room, he noticed things he hadn't before. Like nail pops in the walls near the doorway into the kitchen and scuffed paint on the baseboards. The bookshelf next to the fireplace looked crooked, and he rose to check it out.

"Careful," Carrie warned. "It's getting a little wobbly. I need to get that fixed before Aviva pulls a book off the shelf and the entire thing topples."

"This is dangerous," he stated, looking around to see if there was something to secure the bookcase. "Don't leave her alone in this room."

Carrie's eyes flashed. "I know how to take care of my niece."

He realized how his comment had come across at about the same time Carrie blushed.

"I'm sorry," he said, softening his tone.

"I am, too," she added. "I didn't mean to jump on you. You're right about the bookcase. In fact, I've got a list of the repairs I need to make around here. I'm still getting used to being in a small town where everyone is in everyone else's business."

She held up her hands in apology. "Not that I object to your help in keeping her safe. Do you know any reputable repairmen?"

He nodded. "I get it. At the risk of making you even more uncomfortable, would you let me help out with that list of repairs? Isaac tried to help me, and I brushed him off. I can't apologize to him, but it would make me feel better if I could work on his list. It's a way for me to make amends, I guess?"

"Of course," Carrie said, a look of relief on her face. "That would really help me out. And how about, as a thank-you, I make you some of my famous Hanukkah *bimuelos*?"

He grinned, patting his stomach. "I wouldn't refuse."

* * *

Carrie looked around the living room, trying to see it through Arlo's eyes. He was right; there were a lot of things that needed minor repairs. Randi had decorated it with an eye toward hominess and comfort—light gray walls, green and blue pillows on the sofa, colorful family photos on the white fireplace mantle and wood furniture stained a dark gray. It was calming and definitely family friendly, but, as Arlo pointed out, things needed repairing. Even Isaac had kept a list in his desk of repairs that needed to be made. She was happy to accept Arlo's help, especially if it meant he'd be around more often.

Just watching him with her niece gave her a sense of joy she'd missed these last few weeks. Aviva clearly loved him, and he seemed to return the feelings. Right now, he'd moved onto the floor with the toddler, handing her blocks for her to build a tower. She'd build it, knock it down and chortle with glee.

Carrie settled back onto the sofa, content to watch the two of them together while she got some of her own work done. The more often he was here to fix things, the more he and Aviva could continue to strengthen their bond. Without a father, it was more important than ever for her niece to have a strong male figure in her life.

And Arlo was definitely strong. He might be involved with the business side of the ranch, but his forearms were muscular, his shoulders wide, and he appeared to handle any physical tasks she gave him with ease. But as much as she admired his outward strength, there was more to him than met the eye. He was confident and clearly willing to put his own work and troubles aside to help others. Those were traits she admired, but she didn't want whatever was bothering him to fester. Maybe if she spent more time with him, she'd be able to convince him to investigate the relationship between his father and Stevie Fields. Because as she'd written time and again in her articles, true peace didn't happen until a person had worked through an issue. And the only way that would happen for Arlo was if he stopped running from what "might be."

Not to mention, focusing on helping Arlo helped her gain control of her own grief.

Aviva started rubbing her eyes, and with a start, Carrie realized it was nap time.

"Hey, baby girl, it's time to go *durme*."

Arlo frowned in confusion.

"It's Ladino for sleep," Carrie said. "Ladino is a combination of Hebrew and Spanish."

He shook his head. "That's so interesting."

Aviva held out her arms to him. "Arwo."

Carrie wasn't sure who melted more, her or Arlo. All she knew was her own heart turned to mush as the muscular man lifted the sweet child into his arms, cradling her against his broad chest as she rested her head on his shoulder and stuck her thumb in her mouth.

She must have sighed out loud, because Arlo glanced her way. Her pulse raced at the look he gave her, like they were part of something. Together. Blinking, suddenly thrown into something she didn't quite recognize, she blurted, "I'll show you the way."

As soon as the words escaped her lips, she flushed. He'd been here before, so surely, he knew which way was Aviva's bedroom.

His eyes glowed, like he smiled from within, but instead

of correcting her, he simply whispered to Aviva, "Which animal should I be today?"

Her niece answered in a sleepy voice. "A sheep."

As Arlo bahhed his way out of the living room and upstairs to Aviva's bedroom, Carrie struggled to collect herself. This man who was so aloof was perfectly fine turning himself into an animal to please a two-year-old? And somehow, in the process, he made her feel she was part of their special group.

Because the two of them—this man who seemed to appear right when she needed him, and this little girl who brightened up even Carrie's darkest day—had a bond.

While Carrie pulled down the blackout shades in Aviva's duck-themed room and made sure her toddler bed with the white eyelet cover was ready for the nap, Arlo deposited the child on the floor before getting down on all fours and continuing to play the sheep. He nudged her with his face, making her giggle. Once she climbed into bed, Arlo suggested he read her a story.

Carrie sat in the maple rocker—the same one their mom had used when she and her sister were babies—and listened while he told Aviva a story about a lamb who was looking for just the right spot of grass to snack. Every place she nosed, she didn't like. One area was too minty, another too mossy, until finally she found the perfect blades of grass, under a tree where after she ate, she could nap.

By the time he finished reading, Aviva lay curled in her bed, eyes drooping, thumb in her mouth. Carrie didn't know whether to laugh at his antics or ask him to teach her how he did it. Her niece never went down as easily for her.

They left the room together, and, in the hallway, she spoke to him. "You are the toddler whisperer," she said.

He shrugged. "Toddler whisperer, ranch whisperer, I'll take whatever you'd like to call me."

"You're clearly multi-talented."

He followed her into the kitchen and waited while she put a kettle on to boil.

"Isaac used to call me ranch whisperer because I have a knack for turning struggling ranches around."

"Randi told me. I heard you and your family recently bought a ranch on the other side of town."

He nodded. "We did. And I'm doing my thing and making sure it's as successful as possible for our family."

She handed him a mug. "Isaac used to talk about you, you know. Said you were the only finance guy he'd trust, other than himself."

"That was mighty nice of him." He paused for a moment, before walking around Carrie and opening the cabinet above her.

The position of his body hemmed her in and made her aware of him as a man. He smelled like pine and soap, reminding her of her grandmother's kitchen during Passover cleaning. She would have taken a deep breath, but her lungs were constricted by his large presence. Hyperaware of him, the hairs on the back of her arm rose as his biceps came within an inch of her. He never touched her, but his proximity did things to her. Things she shouldn't think about, not when she was alone in the house with a toddler to take care of.

His breathing echoed in her head, making strands of her hair billow. It would be easy to lean back, just a fraction, to feel his body against hers—hard muscle, soft fabric, prickly whiskers. She'd been strong and on her own for so long. All she wanted was to give in for one minute.

What would he do if she leaned back? Or better yet, turned around and let their bodies touch?

Then his stomach rumbled, and the spell was broken. She closed her eyes, grateful she hadn't given in to her weakness...or her desire. This was Arlo, her brother-in-law's best friend. He was here because of Aviva. Just like him, her focus needed to be on her niece.

"I thought we might need plates," he said, his voice gravelly. "In case you wanted a snack to go along with your tea."

Did all men think only about food or was it just Arlo? "I guess you're hungry," she murmured.

Turning, she met his green-eyed gaze. Once again, the color seared itself into her brain, reminding her of Lake Chatelaine on a stormy day, when the wind whipped up and the sky turned that greenish-yellow gray right before a tornado.

What kinds of thoughts were racing through his brain to turn his eyes that color? They couldn't be just for food, could they?

He remained silent long enough for her to realize she was right, he wasn't thinking only about food. Carrie replayed her comment in her head, and her body heated. She suspected her face was turning red.

Lovely.

He stepped away and finally responded, "I could eat."

Thank goodness.

The situation was slipping away from her, something she couldn't afford to let happen. She poured tea into the two mugs and slid them toward Arlo while she searched the fridge for snacks. The refrigerated air cooled her cheeks, and by the time she'd pulled out hummus, cheese and cut-up vegetables, she felt more in control. Grabbing pita crackers from the pantry, she arranged everything onto a tray and brought it back into the living room.

His eyes widened. "I didn't mean for you to go to such trouble."

"No trouble. Besides, this is what happens when you tell a Jewish woman you're hungry." *Or when she needs a minute to collect herself.*

"Noted," he said. He dipped a raw carrot into the hummus and stuck it in his mouth. Her throat dried as she watched his strong jaw and throat move as he chewed and swallowed.

So much for cooling off and collecting herself.

"Have you put up your Christmas tree yet?" she asked, searching for a topic of conversation to distract herself.

He sipped his tea before shaking his head. "I'm skipping the tree this year."

Carrie was taken aback. "Why?"

"I'm not in a festive mood, no matter how many ads I see, or how many stores try to convince me to get into the Christmas spirit. I don't think half of them would recognize the meaning of the holiday if they fell over it."

He couldn't really mean to skip Christmas, could he?

"I've noticed Chatelaine is really getting into the holiday spirit," she said. "All the restaurants and stores are decorated and—"

"Don't forget the sales," he said, his voice bitter. "It's not Christmas if you can't spend money on things no one needs. I swear," he said, "people become like my dad at this time of year, so caught up in the materialistic side..."

His hands were fisted on the table, and he wasn't looking at her, but off into the distance. His body was taut with tension.

She wanted to reach across and cover his hand with hers, to ease whatever was troubling him. But she didn't know him well enough, and besides, he might not want that. Just because his attitude about Christmas made her feel bad didn't mean she could assume she knew what was best. She gripped her mug of tea tighter.

He shook his head. "Sorry about that. You didn't deserve that outburst."

She blew on the tea before answering. "You don't have to apologize to me," she said. "It is easy to get caught up in shopping during the holidays and forget about the meaning behind it. I get it. I'm responsible for Aviva's Hanukkah celebrations this year—both the religious rituals and the fun, present-y ones, and there's a huge side of me that wants to buy her everything I see." Part of that desire was to make up for what she'd lost, as if somehow a toy could make losing her parents less awful.

"What stops you?" His gaze bore into her.

"You mean besides the fear of bankruptcy?" she deadpanned.

He huffed in response, his gaze brightening.

She smiled and continued. "I keep thinking about the meaning of the holiday and how Randi asked me to help teach Aviva about her heritage. Hanukkah's a pretty minor holiday, but it has lots of traditions. So, although I will buy her presents, there are so many other activities that we'll be doing, and I'm trying to focus on all of them."

He nodded. "As I mentioned before, I know a little about Hanukkah," he said. "Mostly that potato pancakes are delicious. Although," he paused. "Isaac and Randi always invited me to dinner the last night of Hanukkah."

She laughed. "Clearly the way to your heart is through

your stomach. That dinner is called a *merenda*." His gaze intensified, and she looked away before continuing. "Although I already told you the story of Hanukkah, I'm happy to teach you, along with Aviva, more about the holiday, especially since you'll probably be here during a lot of our activities. Your first lesson," she said with a smile, "is that it is about way more than potato pancakes. I'll have to make you some *cassola* and *keftes de espinaca*. They are delicious!"

He pushed his plate away and leaned back on the sofa. "I think I've had those, but I'd love to learn. And clearly, I'm going to have to drag out the repairs needed around here, since I need to try all the food, even though I don't understand half of what you're saying."

Carrie laughed, glad to see Arlo's mood changing. She hadn't been sure she'd be able to dredge up enough holiday spirit to teach her niece, but maybe she could help the two of them and herself at the same time.

"*Cassola* is a sweet cheese pancake and *keftes de espinaca* are spinach patties. Sephardic Jews make them at Hanukkah because they're deep-fried in oil."

Arlo patted his stomach. "Sounds good to me. I'll take as many as you want to make me."

She took a sip of tea and replaced the mug on the table again. "On second thought, maybe I'll teach you to make them." There was nothing sexier than a man cooking. Her cheeks heated, and she brushed the thought away. "In fact, why don't you come for dinner one night this week? We can have a mini-Hanukkah food-making lesson, and then you can try all the delicacies. And maybe tell me a little about your Christmas celebrations."

Oh, gosh, had she gone too far? Her only intent had

been to make him feel better and to get him to want to participate in the holidays.

But the smile that lit him from within eased her fears. "I'd like that."

Her stomach fluttered with excitement at the thought of dinner with Arlo. "Great," she said. "And thank you."

He frowned. "For what?"

"You're helping me get into my own holiday spirit."

Rising from the sofa, he brought the tray of snacks into the kitchen. She followed him, and almost bumped into him when he turned. He held on to her arms to keep her from falling over. His scent, his proximity, his touch, sent shivers down her spine. Time stopped as he looked at her, his thumbs making circles on her skin. The silence lengthened. She licked her suddenly dry lips, and like the crack of a starter pistol, he pulled back.

"Anything I can do to help." One corner of his mouth turned up before he grabbed his hat and left her house.

The short drive to his brother Ridge's house was not nearly enough time for Arlo's thoughts to settle. Indeed, his heart still pounded, and his palms were slick on the steering wheel as he thought about how close he'd come to kissing Carrie.

Kissing Carrie.

It had been the only thought potent enough to cut through his bitterness. As far as he was concerned, the holidays should be canceled this year. He was in no mood to celebrate them or humor the commercialization gods.

He'd even let some of his feelings bleed into his conversation with Carrie. But somehow she'd managed to wiggle past his defenses, show her compassion and entice him all at once. From the moment he'd entered her kitchen, all he'd wanted to do was take her in his arms and kiss her.

Was that even allowed? She was still in mourning for her sister. Yet he'd swear she'd looked at him like she wanted to kiss him, too. She smelled like flowers, and being near her had made all his rational thoughts evaporate.

He shook his head as he turned off the ignition. He was supposed to be helping Carrie, not jumping her bones, no matter how enticing she might be. This wasn't the time to start something with her.

He stayed inside his truck for another a minute, thinking about her. The woman amazed him. In the face of all her hardship, she was still able to look forward and find joy. And despite his initial protests about the holiday, she'd even made him eager to celebrate pieces of it with her. How did she do it? Maybe it was the responsibility of taking care of a child. Because she took that responsibility seriously. It would have been easy for her to do what was best for herself, regardless of her sister's wishes. But she was intent on carrying out her promise to Randi and Isaac and celebrate the holiday, no matter how sad she was.

He shook his head. Responsibility might explain Carrie's eagerness for Hanukkah, but he had responsibilities, too, and they were doing nothing to get him in the holiday mood. Helping ensure his family's ranch success was hard work. When his mother had bought the ranch, he'd been all for working here, as had his siblings. But instead of giving him joy, all the ranch did was remind him of his father and his best friend. Every success he had on the Fortune Family Ranch made him want to say, *"See, Dad?"* It also made him want to go out and celebrate with Isaac or ask his financial advice. He had to find a way forward, but he didn't know how. That's why he'd driven to his brother's house.

He looked through the windshield toward Ridge's cabin. Two stone square pillars with a plain bronze-looking gate sat at the entrance to his gravel driveway. The gate and pillars were similar to his own in simplicity, although Arlo's stone pillars were lower and wider, and his gate was wood. Since the family owned the entire thirty-five-hundred-acre ranch, they rarely kept the gates closed, and Arlo drove right through.

He pulled his pickup truck up to his brother Ridge's cabin. Similar to his own, the center part of the structure was a wooden A-frame, with wings on either side and a large front porch that faced the ranch. But he knew from experience that the back of the house was the impressive part, with almost an entire wall of windows overlooking Lake Chatelaine.

He climbed out of his truck and grabbed his hat. Maybe Ridge could help. As kids, they'd stuck together. As teenagers, they'd gotten into trouble together. And as adults, they'd looked to each other for advice. When Arlo had a problem, he'd always talked to his younger brother. But still, he didn't move. Somehow, when faced with the need to do something to solve his problems, paralysis struck.

He scoffed. Sitting in his truck wasn't helping matters. With a sigh, he climbed out, grabbed his Stetson and made his way up to the front door.

Like everyone else, his brother's cabin was decorated for Christmas, with a big wreath on the front door. He knocked on Ridge's door, all the while wondering what outdoor decorations, if any, Carrie planned for her house for Hanukkah. He hadn't asked her about decorating. He'd have to remember to do that tomorrow.

A female voice to his left startled him.

"Hi," Hope, the woman who was staying with Ridge while she recovered from losing her memory, greeted him. She held her seven-month-old daughter, Evie, in her arms.

"Hi, Hope," Arlo said. "How are you?"

She gave a shy smile. "Okay, thanks. You?"

"Pretty good," he answered.

The front door swung wide, and Ridge answered the door.

"Arlo." The two men slapped each other's backs. "Come on in," Ridge said. He looked at his auburn-haired house-guest and an expression passed across his face. "Hope, did you need anything?"

"No, I was just going to go to the grocery store. I'm out of milk."

"I've got plenty inside. Come on in." He made room for Hope and the baby to pass by him, before addressing Arlo. "You just caught me. I was about to go back out and talk to Bender about sheepherding. Can I get you anything?"

Arlo shrugged. "I just wanted to say hello." He watched Hope head into the kitchen, noticing how similar she looked from the back to Carrie when she held Aviva. They both turned their faces into the baby, they both arched their backs the same way. Maybe it was a mom thing, even if Carrie wasn't quite a mom.

"What's up, Arlo?" Ridge's expression changed from fondness as he looked at Hope to concern as he focused on him.

His brother cared for that woman.

Arlo shook his head and paced around the room. He'd

loved being with Carrie, but now he was antsy and didn't know why.

"My head's just in a weird place, you know?"

Ridge nodded. "It's only been a month since Isaac died, and less than a year since Dad did. Your head is going to be messed up for a while."

"I shoulda made peace with Dad before he died. And now…" He shrugged.

"Why didn't you?"

This was a mistake coming here. He couldn't tell Ridge, or any of his siblings, what he'd found in that box. It would mess up those who'd made amends with the man, and not help those who hadn't. He had to shoulder this burden alone.

"Stubborn, I guess." He needed to change the subject. His gaze bounced off the Christmas tree in the other room.

"What are you getting Hope and Evie for Christmas?"

Ridge held his finger to his lips before pulling out his phone and showing Arlo a picture of a diamond key pendant.

Arlo grinned. "That's beautiful, but a little fancy for a seven-month-old."

His grin faded as Ridge nudged him with his shoulder. "Jerk."

Rubbing it, he nodded. "Nice. And how about the baby?"

"That's more Hope's department."

"What's Hope's department?" Hope asked as she returned to the great room. She handed Evie to Arlo while she poured the milk into a bottle.

Arlo shook his head when she reached for Evie again. "That's okay, I like holding her. Right, Evie?"

Evie gurgled and gave him a big smile.

His chest warmed. Something about babies always made

him feel good. It was weird. He'd never have thought of himself as a baby lover, but between Evie and Aviva…

"I was asking what you're getting Evie for Christmas."

Hope's face brightened. "It's her first one, so I want it to be special. But she's so young, it's not going to mean much to her. Probably a couple of cute outfits and a toy or two."

Ridge turned to her. "Maybe more than a toy or two, but we'll see."

Hope looked up at him and smiled.

An idea crossed his mind. "I don't suppose you'd know what to get a two-year-old for Hanukkah?" He wasn't sure where that question came from, but suddenly, he wanted to add Aviva, and maybe even Carrie, to his holiday list.

Hope's eyes brightened. "Two-year-olds are fun, and with eight days of gifts, you could buy all sorts of things," she said. "You could get developmental toys, like puzzles, or stacking toys. Books are always good, too, like *The Very Hungry Caterpillar* or *Goodnight Moon*. Or even a stuffed animal—"

She froze, and, confused, Arlo glanced at Ridge in alarm, while squeezing Evie against his chest.

"Hope, what's wrong?" Ridge asked.

Her eyes were wide, but she remained silent, as if she was somewhere else. Seconds ticked by, with Arlo watching Ridge as his face crinkled in concern.

Finally, she blinked, before reaching for Ridge and burying her face in his shoulder. Her shoulders rose and fell while they waited for her to speak. Finally, she turned, tears in her eyes.

"I remembered being in a man's embrace," she whispered. "I was loved, cherished." She touched the ring finger on her left hand. "I was wearing a wedding ring."

Arlo glanced at his brother. Ridge's face was white, his throat working convulsively. Sympathy washed over Arlo. His brother cared for Hope, but if she was married… Where was her husband? Would she remember who he was and leave?

Arlo looked at her bare ring finger. How come there wasn't a ring? Did she take it off? Why?

That question hung in the air, suspended in the kind of fragile shield no one dared break. But from the glances between Ridge and Hope, he knew that question was top of mind.

Arlo shouldn't be here. He should leave them to deal with this together, without any interference. Except he was holding Evie, and handing her back to them might draw more attention to his presence. The baby was drinking her bottle in peace, and it was one less thing they had to deal with right now.

So, he sat at the table in silence, wondering how Ridge could handle not knowing Hope's background. Knowing at any moment this life he was considering with her could come crashing down around him. How did he wrap his head around the magnitude of unfinished business? As usual, it was another lesson for him, if only he could learn from it. But he couldn't ask his brother for advice. Not now, while he was in the thick of it. That wouldn't be fair.

Ridge and Hope stood together for a few moments more, before separating and looking at Arlo apologetically.

"I'm sorry," she said. "These memories come back at the most unexpected, and inconvenient, times. What were we discussing? Oh, right, gifts." She gave him a weak smile, and his heart broke for her.

"No, no, it's fine," he said.

She reached for Evie, and he handed the baby back to her, taking care not to dislodge the bottle.

"I should leave you two alone," he said, rising.

His brother gave him a grateful look and led him to the front door.

"Thanks, man. I'm sorry about that," Ridge said.

Arlo took him by the shoulders. "You have nothing to apologize for. Neither does she. You're both in an impossible situation. Go be with her. I'm okay."

"You sure?"

Of course not. But he couldn't tell his brother that. A vise tightened around his chest. His brother and Hope, Carrie and Aviva. They were all grieving, trying to find their way. He was, too. How was he supposed to help any of them if he couldn't even help himself?

Chapter Four

The rest of Carrie's day passed in a fog, as thoughts of Arlo consumed her. *Anything* he could do to help? *Help?* What exactly did he mean? She threw laundry into the washer, wondering if he was volunteering to clean her clothes. She blushed as she hung her lingerie to air dry. *No thank you, sir. Or maybe yes, please.* Jeez, how desperate was she to jump into a full-on flirtation with the first guy who caught her eye. She was here for a reason, not a vacation.

Sitting at her computer and working on an article on vitamins for her health and wellness sites, her mind lingered on Arlo. Or rather, his stomach. He loved to eat. What vitamins did he take? Did he work out? He was trim, and she'd admired his muscles at various times. She'd assumed he got them from ranch work, yet he claimed to mostly be involved in the behind-the-scenes office work. Like Isaac. Did he go to a gym? Or work out at home? A vision of him with sweat trickling, muscles defined, skin flushed, came to mind, and she fanned herself. This was ridiculous.

When Aviva woke from her nap, Carrie read her a story about a dreidel. But instead of seeing the brightly colored pictures on each page, she visualized scenes from their time together this morning—every look Arlo had given her, every clearing of the throat, every brush of his body against hers.

She shook her head to clear it.

"No, no, no," Aviva said, shaking her head also.

Carrie laughed, and the little imp repeated the action.

She swung her up in the air and blew on her belly. They descended into silliness, and slowly, Carrie's tension faded away.

Deciding to take advantage of the good weather, she brought Aviva outside to play. Isaac and Randi had put up a play set in the backyard, one of those timber ones with two swings, a slide and a little playhouse at the top. She pushed her niece in the baby swing, watching her cackle with glee and yell "higher" with each push.

Once again, her thoughts turned to Arlo, but this time, she was more rational. Maybe she was reading too much into it. Sure, he was good-looking, and yes, there might have been some chemistry between them, but probably not as much as she imagined. The man was in mourning, just like she was. Who was it who said, "Don't make any decisions within the first six months of someone close to you dying"? Well, he'd lost his father and his best friend. If he was interested in her at all, it was probably for a quick fling, and while she was flattered, it wasn't what she needed right now. She needed to focus on Aviva and on getting all of the legal paperwork completed for adopting her niece. She also had to figure out how to make a stable home for the child and somehow learn to live without her sister. Arlo was a great friend, and she was happy to try to help him deal with his grief. But anything more than that just wasn't in the cards.

Her phone rang, and she put in her earpods.

"Hey, Emma, how did your show go?" Emma was an artist, and she'd had her first gallery showing in Albuquerque last week. Carrie had wanted to be there, but it hadn't worked out.

"It went great! People actually showed up, other than just my family."

"Woo-hoo, that's terrific!" Carrie said.

"Woo-hoo," Aviva cried.

"Did you hear that?" Carrie laughed. "My niece agrees with me. And I don't know why you're surprised. Your art is amazing."

"Thanks. A couple people bought some of my prints, and the gallery agreed to display the rest for another month."

"Oh, I'm so happy for you, Em. I wish I could have seen it. Maybe when I come home…" She pushed Aviva on the swing.

"Are you still planning to come home in the New Year?"

Carrie paused before answering. "As soon as I get everything settled here."

"Oh, I sense a hesitation in your voice," Emma said. "What's going on?"

"Nothing, why?"

"Because any other time we've talked, you've been wholeheartedly set on coming home ASAP. But you hesitated just now. Why?"

Had she? "Aviva's life is here…"

Emma's voice gentled. "She's two, Carrie. She'll be okay wherever you are. Have you met people? Kelsey said she keeps pushing you to make friends."

"Just a guy—"

"Aha! That's why you hesitated," Emma crowed. "Okay, tell me about him."

"It's not like that, Em. Arlo was good friends with Isaac and is great with Aviva."

At the mention of her name, the child turned her head and looked at Carrie.

Carrie smiled at her, phone balanced on her shoulder.

"And?" Emma stopped talking, forcing Carrie to fill in the silence.

She hated when that happened.

"And I feel bad for him because he's going through loss, too."

"What else?"

"What do you mean?" she asked.

"I mean what's he look like, do you like him, all the juicy details. Come on, I'm an artist. I'm a visual person."

Carrie laughed despite her annoyance. "He's good-looking. Tall, muscular, sandy blond hair. Green eyes." She disappeared into images her mind created until Emma brought her back to the present.

"So, he's a gorgeous cowboy and you're falling for him."

"What? No, I'm not! I don't have time to fall for him, Em. I have too many changes in my life going on right now. The last thing I need is a gorgeous cowboy."

"Says you," Emma said. "I think a gorgeous cowboy is exactly what you need."

The next day, Arlo woke up early, after not getting much sleep the night before. His mind had been racing with what ifs. What if he'd made peace with his dad? What if he found out the truth about the box of toys?

What if he'd kissed Carrie?

After being woken from a dream in which a rodeo's worth of bucking broncos jumped out of the box of toys and trampled Arlo's siblings to death, he sat up drenched in sweat and decided to get out of bed. He dressed in jeans and a work shirt and trod barefoot into his home office. Sitting behind his desk, eyes gritty, he texted Ridge to check in. After yesterday, he wanted to be sure his brother was okay. Then he followed up with Nash about bringing Ridge in to help him learn more about ranch management, especially on the horse side of the ranch. They also discussed Nash's strategic three-year plan for the ranch.

By ten in the morning, he'd finished his immediate work and was ready to head over to Carrie's house to start on her repairs. While he was there, he'd see if he could tell if any of Hope's gift suggestions might work. Yawning, he added stopping for coffee to his list and drove over to the Daily Grind, across the two-lane highway from the Longhorn Feed & Seed.

Inside, he waved hello to Miss Callie, the owner, who was serving one of her famous apple pies, and glanced across the dining room to the back corner. Sure enough, Beau Weatherly sat at his usual table with a sign, Free Life Advice. He scoffed. The man was great and all, but this is how he chose to spend his retirement? At age thirty, retirement was rarely on his mind, but Arlo knew that when he eventually stopped working, he wasn't going to spend his free time sitting in a coffee shop spouting life's wisdom to others.

He stood at the front counter and pointed to his coffee cup, waiting until Sylvie, the waitress, filled it. Then again, Beau was smart and friendly. And he'd been a successful investor. Maybe he'd have a suggestion for him.

Silently calling himself every ridiculous name he could think of, he headed over to Beau's table.

"Mind if I join you?" Arlo asked.

The old man's face creased in a smile. "Not at all." He swept his arm across the gingham tablecloth toward the empty seat, and Arlo sat. They drank their coffee in silence for a little while as he gathered the nerve to talk to a stranger about his problems.

But talking to those he knew didn't seem to help. Isaac's letter, the box of toys he intercepted, his dad, Carrie. Everything weighed him down, and he didn't know where to start.

He sighed. "Beau, what would you say if I told you I was right about something—"

Beau laughed. "You sure you want my advice, or should we just jump to the end where we shake hands?"

Arlo laughed. "Really?" He raised an eyebrow.

"Hey, my advice may be free, but that doesn't mean it doesn't come without commentary."

"Maybe I should rephrase," Arlo said.

"Go ahead, I'm listening."

"I have a problem, but I'm afraid if I pursue it, I'll open a can of worms and make things worse. If I'm right, nothing is going to come out of stirring things up unnecessarily. But if I'm wrong, which I don't think I am, I might find peace. But I don't know if it's worth potentially hurting others."

Beau grunted before taking another drink of his coffee. He flagged down the waitress, who topped both mugs off before leaving them alone again.

"Well, son, I'm a big believer in leaving well enough alone."

Arlo's chest lightened.

"However, this doesn't sound like one of those times."

Shoulders slumping, Arlo waited.

"The truth is everything. You sound completely torn up. And I don't think you're going to get closure, or find peace, or get that horse back into the barn, until you pursue whatever it is that's troubling you."

Goddammit.

He was afraid, and he hated being afraid. But he hated being stubborn more. He sipped his coffee, thinking if his family could read his thoughts...

That would be awful. He *was* headstrong, but that trait had made him a successful investor. He knew which things and ideas to stick with, even when others would have abandoned them long ago. But when stubbornness prevented him from moving forward?

His brothers and sisters had often accused him of that, and maybe they were right.

Beau chuckled softly behind his mug of coffee. "Hurts when you have to admit you're wrong, doesn't it?"

What, the man was a mind reader, too?

"It's not that I don't want to admit I'm wrong," Arlo said. "It's just I'm not used to it. I know that sounds terrible, and I don't mean to be all holier-than-thou. But usually, I'm a good judge of character, of what ideas have potential and what ones don't. So, it's hard for me to take a step back."

Isaac used to help him with this. He'd been his sounding board, keeping him in line when he'd been inclined to chase his idea a little too far. His bullheadedness had cost him the last month of his best friend's life. If ever there was a time to make an adjustment, this was it.

Beau nodded. "It's always harder to change yourself than it is to change others."

Arlo put his coffee cup down on the table, reached into his pocket for his wallet and put a twenty down.

"You're right. I have to find out the truth, no matter how painful it might be. Coffee's on me today, Beau. Thank you."

Beau nodded again and smiled at Arlo as he left the coffee shop.

Arlo couldn't ask his dad about Stevie. The only way to find out the truth and get closure was to go hunt the little boy down.

Outside, he was about to climb back in his truck when the bright-colored display window of the GreatStore caught his eye. The store carried everything. Surely it would have something he could get Aviva. Thinking about Hope's suggestions for Hanukkah gifts, he entered.

The store was festooned with Christmas decorations. Above the door was a huge wreath with red and white bells. Silver garlands outlined the doorway, and white lights surrounded each of the huge picture windows. The checkout lanes had red garlands wrapped around the number poles. Christmas tunes played over the loudspeaker. There was a giant sled filled with wrapped gifts in green, red and gold, with a sign that said This Way to Santa. A huge section of the store had been organized with everything you could possibly need for the holiday, including an entire aisle of trees and ornaments. Even the employees were dressed up like Santa's elves. For the first time, Arlo paused. What must it be like being Jewish, or any other religion for that matter, when everyone around you celebrated Christmas in such an in-your-face way? Isaac had never complained about it, at least not to him. Randi hadn't mentioned anything to him, either, but he was starting to understand why Randi had made a point of making Carrie in charge of teaching Aviva about her religion. As he walked through the store toward the toy aisle, he realized how hard it must be for her.

He wandered the aisles, paying special attention to the toys. There were several toddler toys that looked age appropriate, but he couldn't remember if Aviva had them or not. He'd have to investigate while he was at their house today. The store had an aisle dedicated to books of all kinds, with mostly bestselling books for adults, but there were also a few rows of children's volumes. Again, there were a few board books, including titles Hope had mentioned, and Arlo made a mental note to check what Aviva already had. Maybe Remi's Reads had more. Just as he was about to leave, he noticed a small display of bright-colored dreidels. He stopped, pleased.

One of the elf salespeople must have noticed his shock, because she pointed to them with a smile. "The colorful tops are so pretty, aren't they?"

He didn't bother to correct the young worker but nodded and walked forward to take a closer look. There were all different kinds and sizes and styles of dreidels. Some of them, on their own, were beautiful pieces of artwork—ceramic with painted flowers, or wooden with carvings. Before meeting Carrie, he probably never would have stopped to take more than a cursory glance, but now, they piqued his interest.

"Do you think any of these would be good for a two-year-old?" he asked the elf.

"What about this one," she said, holding up a colorful wooden one.

"Perfect." Arlo paid for the dreidel and returned to his truck.

When he arrived at Carrie's house, he took his toolbox and the bagged dreidel from the cab and rang the doorbell.

"Hey," Carrie said, answering after a few moments. "Come on in."

He removed his hat upon entering and hung it from the hook before handing the bag to her. "I saw this in a store and thought of Aviva," he murmured. "Is it okay if I give it to her before I get started working?"

Carrie's face lit up, and Arlo was struck with not only how pretty she was in her simple jeans and light blue top, but also how easy it was to make her happy. The dreidel wasn't an expensive gift. It wasn't even for her. But the expression on her face made it seem like he'd dedicated a brand-new, prize-winning heifer in her honor.

"This is wonderful!" she exclaimed. "Where did you find it?"

Arlo stuffed his hands in his pockets. "The GreatStore in town."

"I had no idea they carried Hanukkah merchandise." She gave him a hug. "It's so nice of you to pick it out for her. Of course, you can give it to her."

Arlo remained standing in place, still wrapped up in her floral scent and the feel of her arms around him. Her hug was spontaneous and…intoxicating. He would have liked it to last longer, to see what holding her felt like. But she'd released him and backed up, only making him realize it had happened after the fact. So, if it was so quick, why did he miss her? At her curious stare, he mentally gave himself a shake. He was making more of it than was meant. Clearing his throat, he took the dreidel back from her and followed her into the living room.

Once again, Aviva sat on the floor in orange leggings and an orange and purple top, playing with her toys.

"Vivie, look what Uncle Arlo has for you," Carrie said.

"Arwo," the toddler cried, standing up and running over to him.

"What's cookin', good lookin'?" he asked, swinging her up over his head and making her giggle.

"Not cookin', pwayin'," Aviva said.

"What are you playing?"

"Wif my toys."

"Your toys? Show me."

He knelt on the floor as Aviva toddled around, picking up different toys and showing them to him. After a couple of minutes, he said, "I have something for you."

She tipped her head to the side, her blond curls tangling across her forehead. With one hand, he brushed her hair out of her eyes. With the other, he held out the bright red wooden dreidel.

"Wed!" she cried. "I wike wed."

"You do?" he asked, pretending to be shocked. "I didn't know that."

"Aviva, do you know what that is?" Carrie asked.

He'd almost forgotten she was there. Craning his neck, he watched her kneel down next to him, take the dreidel and spin it like a top. Aviva's eyes widened, and she lay down on the floor, watching it spin.

"Do it again, pwese," she said.

Carrie repeated the spin. Each time the dreidel landed, she pointed to the Hebrew letter on the side and told Aviva what it was. Arlo paid attention, too. He'd have to ask her about the letters later. For now, he let Carrie lead.

"Arwo spin," Aviva implored.

He and Carrie's gazes met over the toddler's head, and she seemed to ask him if he wanted to without saying a word. Nodding, he took the dreidel in hand and spun it. It didn't spin as well as Carrie's had, but he didn't embarrass himself. When it stopped, Aviva pointed to the letter and said, "Gimel."

"That's right," Carrie said. "Good job! Now you spin."

Aviva took the dreidel, but it skidded across the floor. Frowning, she tried again. After three times, she shook her head and gave it back to Carrie.

Arlo's chest tightened. He hadn't meant to frustrate the child.

But she seemed satisfied having Carrie and him spin, with her calling out the letters. She was smart. Isaac and Randi would be proud.

He looked over at Carrie. She seemed to feel the same if her expression was any clue. She looked at him and nodded. Warmth flooded through him. He'd never had any wordless communication with a woman before, and certainly not twice.

"You want to see something cool?" she asked Aviva.

The toddler nodded.

This time, when Carrie spun the dreidel, she spun it upside down, on its stem, rather than on its bottom. Arlo wasn't sure who was more amazed, Aviva or himself.

"Whoa," he said, as it bounced in the air before spinning and eventually falling to its side.

"Whoa," Aviva mimicked. She clapped her hands, handed the dreidel back to Carrie and said, "Do it again, pwese."

Carrie repeated the trick a few more times before saying, "Okay, no more for now."

Aviva took the dreidel and turned it over in her hands, laying it on its side and yelling out the letter.

"Vivie, are you going to thank Arlo for your gift?"

She raced over to him and squeezed his neck in a hug so hard he couldn't breathe for a second. "Tank you."

"You're welcome."

He'd dallied with them long enough. It was time to get moving on the repairs, but he didn't want to break up the cozy scene they'd created. He sighed to himself as he rose. Didn't matter what he wanted, he'd made a promise, and he was going to keep it.

"Where would you like me to start?" he asked Carrie.

She rose as well. "Actually, could you start in her room? The ceiling fan makes noise when it runs, and I'd like the outlet covers switched to child-safe ones. Plus her closet door is off the track and I can't seem to get it back in line. She loves picking out her own clothes, and I'm afraid she might get her fingers caught."

"No problem."

She led the way upstairs into Aviva's bedroom. He remembered when Isaac was painting it. A pale yellow with ducks along the ceiling, and cows along the bottom.

Arlo walked into the room to see Isaac on the ladder and Randi, one hand on her belly, giving instructions. He laughed.

"I didn't know you were an artist," he said, turning around in a circle.

Isaac shook his head. "Randi's the artistic one. She painted the animals. I'm just the roller dude."

"Roller dude," Arlo said with a chuckle. "You've completely changed him, Randi."

She nodded, a satisfied smile on her face. "One day, Arlo, someone's going to change you, too."

Now, as he followed Aviva, he wondered if he'd ever be as lucky as the two of them were.

"Hewwo, duckies. Hewwo, cows," Aviva said as she walked into the room. "This is my woom," she announced to Arlo.

"I know that, silly. Quack, quack."

Her eyes brightened. "Quack, quack," she replied. "Moooooo!"

He looked around the room and had an idea. "Would you like to be my helper?" he asked Aviva.

She nodded.

After looking over at Carrie for permission—he probably should have asked her first—he set up the step stool that Carrie had provided underneath the fan.

"Can you make sure the step stool doesn't wobble," he asked the toddler. The step stool was secure. There was no way it was going to wobble, not with his weight on it. But Aviva didn't know that.

She nodded again and held on to one side of the stool, her pudgy hands pressed down on it as he got down to business.

Pulling tools from his pocket, he tightened the fan blades, which had come loose and were causing the noise. Careful not to step on Aviva's fingers, he warned her. "Okay, I'm coming down now."

The child pressed against the stool, her face reddening in her efforts. When his feet hit the floor, he knelt down in front of her. "You did great," he praised. "You're a terrific helper."

Aviva jumped up and down, before running over to Carrie and hugging her leg. "I'm helping."

* * *

Carrie looked down at Aviva and tousled her curls. "Yes, you are," she said. "You're doing a wonderful job."

Watching Arlo and Aviva together melted her heart, and although she had her own work to do, she didn't want to move from this spot. No matter how Arlo acted when the holidays were mentioned, he clearly had spirit. His purchase of the dreidel proved it. All they had to do was help him get past his concerns about his father's second family, and Carrie knew he'd enjoy the season.

He turned to her, wiping his hands on his thighs. "What's next?" he asked.

She pulled her gaze away from his thighs. "Let me get my computer," she said. "I made a list."

Before she embarrassed herself further by being caught staring, she walked quickly into the bedroom and grabbed her laptop off the nightstand. Returning to Aviva's room, where Arlo and her niece were once again playing their animal game, she opened up the laptop and pulled up the repair list. She scanned it.

"We should probably move on to the bookcase downstairs that you noticed. Just in case this one gets too close," she said with a smile.

"Right," Arlo said. He looked at Aviva. "Ready to be my helper again?"

Aviva nodded.

"I don't want her getting in your way," Carrie murmured.

"She's not," he answered. "Besides, this way you can also get work done."

This man was so thoughtful. For the first time since her sister died, she didn't feel quite so alone. And letting him help her didn't scare her. In fact, she wanted to help him, too.

They all went back downstairs, and while Arlo set up his tools around the bookcase, Carrie logged onto the health and wellness site. She kept an eye on Aviva, but Arlo had things under control. He and her niece were taking the books off the shelves, and Aviva was helping him make piles. As Carrie worked on her grief article, she was cognizant of the two of them and couldn't help smiling at their bond.

"I spoke to Beau Weatherly this morning," Arlo said, pulling her attention away from her article.

"Who is he again?" she asked.

"He's kind of a town fixture. A kind, older man who sits at his table at the Daily Grind every morning from seven to eight thirty, offering 'free life advice.'" He put finger quotes around the words. "I've never been sure if he was wise or lonely, but after today, I'd have to say wise."

"What advice did you ask him for?"

Arlo paused while he nailed a brace into the bookcase. "There, that should keep it steady," he said. "Just a general question about closure." He gave her a sheepish look. "He also said I needed it."

Carrie paused. She was glad he'd talked to someone about his dilemma. Just as she was learning about herself, sometimes it helped to have an outsider's perspective. Arlo, who was used to taking care of everything and everyone around him, needed time to sort things out.

"You know, you could just google Stevie Fields on Buckers Road and see what comes up," she said. "Or I can—"

"No! I'll do it."

Aviva jumped at Arlo's raised voice.

"Sorry, I didn't mean to shout," he said to both of them. He gave a quick, reassuring smile to Aviva before turning again to Carrie and expelling a deep breath. "I know you're just trying to help. I appreciate it."

Carrie swallowed. She shouldn't have pushed him. Just because she needed control in order to deal with things in her life didn't mean he did. The decision to find out about Stevie Fields should be his alone. "I didn't mean to push you," she began. "I just thought—"

He came over to her. "You didn't do anything wrong." Letting out a sigh, he pulled his phone from his back pocket and sat next to her on the sofa. "It's just that if anyone is going to google the name, it should be me."

Relief filled her. "Of course."

She returned to her article, once again keeping an eye on Aviva and Arlo at the same time, and basically getting nothing done.

He frowned after a couple of seconds.

"The only Fields on Buckers Road I can find is a Lynne Fields. She's probably Stevie's mom and the former mistress of Casper Windham," he ground out. "This is stupid."

"No, it's not," Carrie said. "You don't know who Lynne Fields is. Maybe you're right, but maybe not. And you're never going to know unless you do something about it. Why don't we take the box over to her place right now, tell her it was sent to the wrong address, and see what she says?"

"Okay, okay," he mumbled. "You're probably right."

"What's that?" Carrie asked. "I didn't hear you."

Arlo laughed.

"That's better," Carrie said.

"Alright, I'm out of my funk. And yes, we can go, but not today."

She smiled.

"Or tomorrow," he added.

Instead of feeling frustrated with him, her insides warmed. He was getting there, on his own timetable. Hopefully soon, he'd go through with investigating Stevie Fields and maybe even feel better. In the meantime, this good-looking, kind-hearted man was in her home making the repairs she had yet to get to. She had an adult to talk to, and she was going to make the most of it.

She looked over at Aviva and was delighted when she saw that the child was playing with the dreidel.

"Tell me about your Christmas traditions as a kid," she said, putting aside her laptop.

Arlo stepped back a few feet and examined the bookcase before answering. A faraway look crept onto his face, softening his features and removing all trace of the grumpiness she saw before.

"My mom loves Christmas," he confided. "She was poor and raised by a single mother. They never could do much for Christmas, so when my mom married my dad, she made a huge deal of the holiday, especially as we all came along. My dad, of course, wanted to put on a big show to impress everyone with how rich and successful he was, but my mom kept it personal with little touches she knew we all loved." A brief scowl crossed his face before smoothing out.

"The main Christmas tree, the one my dad insisted on, was professionally decorated. I hated it. But my mom made sure there was another one, a smaller one that we picked out and cut down every year and strung with popcorn and handmade ornaments. Same with our stockings. We each got a stocking that represented our current obsessions or favorite colors. Mine was always blue, even though my dad thought they all should be red and green and matching."

"That sounds lovely," Carrie said. "Were you Christmas Eve opening presents people or Christmas Day?"

His smile stretched wider. "Both."

She laughed. "Really?"

"None of us had any willpower or patience, so we had a kind of white elephant, but with books, on Christmas Eve, and then the rest we opened on Christmas Day."

"Fun! What was your favorite holiday fare?" she asked.

"Anything sweet," he said. "I was never picky, but I guess I favored... Christmas cookies. Honestly, I don't know if it was the taste or what they looked like or just that they meant Santa was coming soon." He patted his totally flat stomach.

Carrie swallowed. She'd never cared much about men's bodies, only their personalities. But looking at Arlo these past few days, and now noticing how his work shirt emphasized his broad shoulders and taut abs, made her wonder what he'd look like shirtless.

And what he'd *feel* like.

"I've always had a weakness for cookies," he confided.

"Cookies?" Aviva looked up eagerly, making them both laugh.

Saved by the toddler.

Carrie wasn't sure if she was relieved or not.

Aviva stood up, tush first, and ran over to Carrie. She placed her hands on Carrie's knees, gave her a big grin and asked, "I have cookies? Pwese?"

"Yes." As she walked with her niece into the kitchen, she said over her shoulder, "See what you did?"

Arlo laughed. "I have no regrets."

He followed them, swinging Aviva into her booster seat and buckling the straps as Carrie pulled out animal crackers from the pantry. She gave her niece apple juice in her yellow sippy cup before leaning over the counter.

"How about a mini latke-making lesson? We can have them for lunch if you'd like to stay."

Carrie's tummy flipped. It wasn't that she didn't want him to stay for lunch, she just hadn't expected to blurt out the invitation like that. Usually, she thought out exactly what she was going to do and say beforehand. But somehow, Arlo made her do things without thinking. And so far, nothing bad had happened with a little spontaneity.

His face split into a wide grin, making his green eyes sparkle.

"I'd love to."

She nodded, not only pleased with his response, but with how easy it happened. Why, she'd think about later.

"Great. First thing is to peel the potatoes. That's your job."

She pulled out several large potatoes from the vegetable bin and handed them to Arlo with a peeler. Folding her arms across her chest, she leaned against the counter, one eye on him, the other on Aviva.

"Wait, you're not going to help me?"

She shook her head. "Don't forget to wash them. And no, that's what you get for creating a cookie monster out of her."

"I didn't realize you were so mean," he said, pretending to pout. He turned on the water and scrubbed the potatoes.

"I'm not mean," she corrected. "Mean would be making you peel the potatoes and not allowing you to eat them."

With a bark that passed for a laugh, he dried the potatoes and began peeling. "Yes, ma'am."

While he peeled, she watched his hands. They were strong, his movements sparse and sure. Before long, he finished. She filled a bowl with cold water and placed the potatoes in it.

"What's that for?" he asked.

"So they don't turn brown."

She plugged in the food processor and then grabbed a large onion from the fridge.

Arlo held up his hands. "Oh, no, don't make me peel those."

Laughing, she took care of it and sliced it into quarters. "No worries, you've redeemed yourself. The first thing we do, after all the peeling, of course, is to alternately shred the potatoes with the onions."

The whirring motor made Aviva cover her ears. To entertain her, Carrie and Arlo did the same thing.

Once they shredded all the potatoes and onions, Carrie added flour, salt, pepper and egg, and mixed the concoction together. Then she placed a large frying pan on the stove, filled it with oil and heated it.

"That's a lot of oil," Arlo remarked.

"I know," she answered, opening the kitchen windows. "If we don't open the windows, the whole house will smell of oil for days."

"Let me help," he said. He finished opening them, before telling her their locks needed repairing as well. While he went to get his toolbox, she waited for the oil to heat.

"Now we drop small amounts into the oil and let them brown."

Carrie made the first batch. When the latkes were just

about ready, she lined a tray with tin foil and then paper towels, before placing the first batch on them to drain and cool.

Arlo reached over to grab one, burning his fingers in the process. It didn't deter him, and he popped a hot one in his mouth.

His eyes widened as he chewed.

"You're going to hurt yourself," she cried, handing him a glass of water.

He gulped it before speaking. "It was worth it," he said. "They're delicious!"

He reached for another, but she shooed his hands away. "Go get applesauce, sour cream, avocados and lox out of the fridge."

That man couldn't be trusted around food, clearly. Someone needed to protect him from himself.

She pointed to the table, and he put out everything he'd gotten from the fridge, along with plates, cups, napkins and silverware.

When he finished, she expected him to try to take another latke. Instead, he stood across the kitchen island, watching her. While his attention was diverted with setting the table, she'd had a nice rhythm going—a forkful of potato mixture, drop into the pan, move the cooking latkes around the pan, flip and remove. But now that he stared at her, her face heated, and she was so distracted that her hands didn't grip the oily spatula as firmly as before, and she dropped a latke on the floor.

He grabbed it. "Five second rule," he said as he popped it into his mouth.

He chewed, emphasizing the cut of his jaw as the muscles worked. He licked his fingers, and her stomach clenched.

She looked away, but not before she caught the twinkle in his eye. *Great, just great.*

"You don't mind that I ate that, do you?" His voice drawled, emphasizing the Texas accent. All he needed to do was add "ma'am" at the end and tip his hat, which was hanging in the hall by the door.

She cleared her throat. "No, I suppose I don't."

Aviva leaned over in her booster seat. "Me want!" she cried, opening and closing her hand as she reached for the latkes.

"Just a minute, sweetheart," Carrie said, arranging the potato pancakes on a serving plate. "They're just about done." She handed the platter to Arlo before rummaging in the fridge for drinks.

Returning with two bottles of water and a sippy cup, she looked around at the table and the two people already sitting at it, waiting expectantly. "Alright, let's eat," she said.

As the three ate latkes, and compared which way they preferred to eat them, Carrie struggled to drag her focus away from his hands, from thoughts about those hands on her... She blinked, and turned toward Aviva, whose face was covered in applesauce, potatoes and grease.

Arlo leaned back in his chair and sighed contentedly. "Mmm, mmm. That was delicious."

Aviva leaned back in her booster seat and imitated his action. "Mmm, mmm."

Carrie and Arlo laughed. They continued to chat as he helped himself to seconds. When he finished, Arlo pushed away from the table and grabbed all three plates. "I'll clean up," he said.

Carrie shook her head. "It's not necessary. You're already fixing things around my house. You don't need to do dishes, too."

He placed his hand over hers. The warmth spread up her arm, and for the first time since her sister died, she felt something other than grief. Hope mingled with red-hot desire.

Glancing into his eyes, she thought she saw a glimmer of the same thing before he blinked.

"You cooked, I do dishes," he said, clearing his throat. "That's the rule."

She frowned. "Whose?"

"Mine."

"But…but what if you don't do it right?" she asked. She gripped the counter and tried to tame her racing heart, suddenly panicking at the loss of control.

He looked at her askance. "Let me get this straight. You trust me to fix things around your house that are falling apart and could hurt you if I do it wrong, but washing dishes and possibly missing a speck or two of grease throws you off?"

He moved closer to her, his large body making her feel tiny. His green eyes pinned her in place, as if convincing her to answer him.

She took a deep breath. When presented his way, it sounded ridiculous. Still, she hated to give up control. It was the one thing that had kept her sane since her sister died. But it was only *dishes*. There was keeping her walls up out of self-preservation and then there was falling down the rabbit hole and never letting anyone do anything for her again. Ever. Plus, it was Arlo, the man who made her insides squishy.

She looked into his endless green eyes and blinked. "I guess when you put it that way…"

While Carrie let Aviva out of her booster seat, Arlo began to wash. "Would you like to inspect?" he asked after washing the frying pan.

Him? Oh, yes.

But he was holding out the pan, and ignoring it would make this already awkward situation even worse.

She took it from him, rubbing her fingers along the surface. No grease. She smiled. "Thank you."

"I'll try not to let my fragile male ego, or my dislike of gender stereotypes, get in the way," he said as he continued washing.

His smirk gave his humor away. It also showed a side of him to Carrie she hadn't expected.

"How about I make it up to you?" she murmured.

He arched an eyebrow. "How?"

"Bimuelos?"

His eyes widened, and he grinned. "You're on."

Chapter Five

As the sun dipped through the trees, Arlo finished fixing the pipe under the master bathroom sink, his mind on Carrie as it had been the entire day. The more time he spent with her, the more he liked her. Aside from being a terrific cook, she was funny and smart. Emotionally strong, too. As he put his tools away, a citrusy sweet smell wafted from the kitchen below, making his stomach growl. He closed his toolbox, peeked into Aviva's room to see if she was there and jogged down the stairs.

He paused in the doorway of the kitchen. Carrie stood at the counter with Aviva sitting next to her. The two of them were patting dough and forming it into balls. He admired the graceful movements of Carrie's arms as she worked the dough. The kitchen light shone onto her dark hair, giving it reddish highlights. And the smile she gave Aviva as the two chatted melted his heart.

He stepped into the kitchen. "I smell something yummy," he said, striding over to Aviva and tickling her tummy.

She giggled and held up her sticky hands. "Bimwos!"

He snagged one, popping it into his mouth and rolling his eyes in delight. "What are you doing this evening?" he asked.

She gave a rueful smile. "Same thing I do every evening.

Putting Aviva to bed and either going through Randi's and Isaac's things or curling up with a book."

Arlo shook his head. "Not tonight you aren't. Tonight, you're going out with me."

She looked at him askance. "Oh, really?"

"Yes, ma'am. Have you seen the lake yet?"

"I've driven by."

He scoffed. "That's a no, then. We're going to the lake."

She pointed out the window. "You do know it's winter, right?"

"Yep."

"And what about Aviva?"

"Bring her."

"But…"

Arlo gripped Carrie's upper arms. They were soft, yet he knew they were strong. Her brown eyes gave away her worry and also, for a split second, desire. Did she want him as much as he was coming to want her? The look was gone before he knew it, but the worry was still there.

"You both deserve a break. And a change of scenery. Please? I promise we'll be back in time for Vivie's bedtime."

He waited, sure she was going to refuse. Just as he was about to let her bow out gracefully, she relented.

"Okay."

Joy surged through him. "I'll pick you up at five."

Pushing away from the counter, he packed up his tools, grabbed a last *bimuelos*—gosh, they were good—and returned to the ranch. He checked in at the office at the main house to make sure there wasn't anything he needed to do right away. And then he got ready for the evening.

At four fifty-eight, he pulled his pickup truck into her driveway. The asphalt needed patching, and he mentally added it to his to-do list. He laughed to himself. If his father could see him now. The man had thought manual labor was beneath him, and here Arlo was, leaning into it. He shook his head to clear it. He didn't want to think about Casper tonight. Glancing into the back seat, he triple-checked there was enough room for Aviva's car seat before getting out of the cab and loping up to Carrie's front door. His hand hovered over the bell, but before he could press it, the door opened.

His heart stuttered. Something about this woman took his breath away. Her shiny brown hair was cascading around her shoulders. She wore jeans that hugged her hips and a V-neck sweater in a light blue color that emphasized her eyes. Her necklace, a gold Jewish star, drew his attention to her chest, but he wasn't about to ogle her. Not when she held Aviva on her hip.

"Arwo!" the toddler cried, holding out her pudgy arms to him.

He took her from Carrie's arms.

"Hello, little one. Hi," he said to Carrie, wondering why he was tongue-tied.

She smiled softly. "Hi."

She reached for a bag with what he presumed was for Aviva, and he took it from her. Their fingers touched, and once again, heat shot up his arm. Their gazes met, and this time he was sure she felt it, too.

"You've got your hands full with her," Carrie said. "I can carry the bag."

"Go open the back seat of the truck," he insisted. "I'll take care of this."

Nodding, she grabbed a jacket from the hook next to

the door, locked the door behind her and rushed over to the truck.

"Pway game?" Aviva asked.

"Hmm," he said as he sat her in her car seat. "We're owls," he said. "Hoot, hoot. They're night animals." He widened his eyes.

"Hoot, hoot," Aviva replied, bugging her eyes out, too.

Arlo opened the door for Carrie, who laughed as she climbed into the truck.

"Okay, owls, it's time to go," she said.

He glanced at the sky through the windshield as he backed out of her driveway. They'd just make it.

"You said the lake," Carrie said. "Where exactly are we going?"

"My cabin."

Out of the corner of his eye, he saw Carrie stiffen.

"Don't worry, we're headed to the dock behind my cabin," he clarified, hoping to put her at ease. The last thing he wanted was for her to think he had anything untoward in mind.

A short time later they arrived at his place and he parked in the driveway. When she unlocked her seat belt, he smiled over at her. "Follow me," he said.

Arlo had chosen his cabin—one of six that he and his five siblings moved into, because of its view of the lake. Entering from the front, he led Carrie through the flag-stone foyer into a huge great room, with the kitchen on the right, a huge sitting area in the center and his office and guest rooms on the left. But it was the back of the house that caused Carrie to gasp.

The back wall was all windows. The views of the lake were spectacular. While she and Aviva stood at one of the windows, he grabbed two blankets and exited the back of his house. Making sure they were still with him, he brought them down to the dock, where two large chairs, made from logs just like his home, sat facing the water. He sat and motioned to Carrie to do the same. When she was settled, he handed her a blanket before pointing to the sky.

"Now watch," he said.

The air was cool, the lake smooth as glass. As the sun began to set, the sky turned shades of pink, red and blue. The colors reflected off the water, turning the world a rainbow hue and making it seem as if the sunset was endless.

"This is…beautiful," Carrie whispered.

The awe in her voice made Arlo smile.

"It is." It's why he'd insisted on a wall of windows at the back. He looked over at her, though, instead of the sunset and thought to himself, *So are you.* He didn't dare say the words out loud. After her stiffening in the car at the idea of going to his house, he didn't to push his luck and scare her off. He watched her snuggle under the blanket with Aviva.

Was it his imagination, or was she sneaking glances over at him, too? In profile in the waning light, it was hard to tell. But a few times, when he thought their gazes may have met, her mouth quirked in a smile. Then again, it could have just been the presence of Aviva. He wasn't sure.

When the sun had set and the colors had muted to black, she turned to him.

"That was one of the most gorgeous sunsets I've ever seen. Thank you." She glanced around the lake for a few more seconds. "You and your neighbors must love living here."

He nodded. "We do."

At her quizzical look, he continued, "The ranch is owned by my family, and my siblings all live on the property, along the lake."

He'd already pointed out Jade's and Nash's houses as they entered the property. "You can't see them from here, but Ridge, Sabrina and Dahlia live farther down. We have golf carts to travel from one cabin to the other."

A wistful expression crossed her face. "It must be nice to live so close to each other."

His heart squeezed with sympathy. What would he do if he lost one of his siblings? He'd thought burying his best friend was awful. He couldn't imagine losing one of his brothers or sisters as well.

"I'm sorry," he said thickly. "I didn't mean to make you sad."

She shook her head, wiping a tear from her cheek.

He made his hand into a fist so as not to catch the tear on his fingertip. He could only imagine how soft her skin would feel.

"It's okay," she said. "I'm glad you brought me here."

He reached across the space between their chairs and squeezed her hand. To his delight, she squeezed back.

"It's getting chilly," he told her. "Would you like to come inside for dinner?" He'd been so sure of himself this afternoon, almost cocky. But now, although still confident, he was aware how skittish she was, and he didn't want to do anything to push her away. So even though she'd agreed to come out with him this afternoon, he checked in with her now, to make sure she was still on board.

He'd bring her home if she wanted…but he hoped she didn't want to leave.

"That would be nice," she replied, her voice shy. She cleared her throat. "I think Aviva is getting cold."

Arlo stood and reached for Aviva, keeping her wrapped in the blanket. With his other hand, he helped Carrie up, and the three of them walked toward his house. He would have liked to hold Carrie's hand longer, but she let go of his, and he didn't try to take it again.

Inside, he lit the fireplace for warmth and then went into the kitchen to check on the beef ribs he'd put in the slow cooker earlier in the day.

Although he wasn't a gourmet chef, he'd wanted a kitchen that was spacious and functional. With red cedar cabinets, copper pendulum light fixtures, black marble countertops and a slate tile backsplash, the room was cozy yet modern. Even Arlo, who didn't like to cook, enjoyed being here. And when he had guests over—usually his family—the open, adjoining dining area and open living area made him feel part of the get-together, even when he had to prepare a meal.

Speaking of which, the barbecue smell wafted up, and he inhaled.

"That smells delicious," Carrie said next to him. "What can I do to help?"

"How about a salad?" He looked across the open kitchen to the living room, making sure Aviva wasn't near the fire. She was sitting on the couch, reading one of the books Arlo kept around for the little ones in his family.

Something about the way her little legs stuck straight forward on his brown leather couch, with the oversize cushions practically swallowing her whole, stirred something in him and made him yearn for a family.

"—you want?"

Carrie's voice startled him, and he turned toward her. She held two heads of lettuce in her hands.

He blinked.

"Which do you want?" Her lips twitched. "In your salad."

"Sorry, wasn't paying attention."

"Clearly."

"Romaine. I think there's Caesar dressing in the cabinet." He walked into the kitchen and reached around her to the pantry. Her hair brushed his nose, and he inhaled the floral scent of her shampoo.

He cleared his throat. "Here you go."

As he handed her the bottle, their hands touched, and this time, he searched her face for a response.

Success! His chest swelled as he watched her bite her lip, her gaze alternating between their fingers and his face in rapid succession.

Despite his desire to continue the contact—keep savoring the warmth of her fingers against his—he let her go, a small smile his only sign that she'd felt the spark, too.

"Thank you," she whispered.

Flashing lights drew Arlo's attention away from Carrie to the slow cooker on the counter.

"Perfect timing," he said, with only a little sarcasm.

He lifted the lid, releasing steam and the aroma of barbecue ribs into the kitchen. Pulling out corn bread warming in the oven, he brought everything to the oak table in the dining room and began setting the table while Carrie finished dressing the salad.

She called Aviva over, got her settled in before taking a look at the food. She closed her eyes and inhaled, then glanced at Arlo, a gleam in her eye.

"Wait a minute. Can you even call yourself a Texan if

you make ribs in a slow cooker? I thought you all were big barbecue people."

He chuckled. "That would be y'all, not you all."

She shrugged. "My question still stands."

Arlo let the silence stretch while he served Carrie so she could cut up the rib meat into bite-size pieces for Aviva. Then he took a bite of his corn bread while formulating his answer.

"Well, you see, yes, Texans love their barbecue, and I'm no different. But we also appreciate reality. And if I'm working all day, I can't devote the proper amount of time to my barbecue, so then I use the slow cooker."

Leaning on her hand, Carrie's eyes widened. "Does that mean you're just like the rest of us mere mortals?"

"Oh, honey, don't you know everything is bigger in Texas?"

Her shoulders shook before she dropped her head and laughed. When she looked at him, tears streamed down her face.

"You cwying?" Aviva asked. Her lip quivered.

"Oh, no, sweetie," Carrie said, quickly wiping her face. "I'm laughing. Arlo made a joke."

The little girl frowned, looking between the two. And then, as if she didn't want to be left out, she laughed, too.

Her forced laughter made Arlo laugh, and Carrie joined in as well.

"All this laughter reminds me so much of the big dinner my family had every Hanukkah," she said, a wistful look on her face. "We'd have my grandparents, aunts, uncles and cousins, and the house was always filled with laughter."

"I've heard of Christmas dinners, but never Hanukkah dinners," Arlo admitted. "What are they like?"

"As I'm sure you've figured out, lots of Jewish holidays revolve around food," she said with a smile. "We have a big celebration the last night of Hanukkah, called a *merenda*, to mark the end of the holiday," she said. "Probably similar, but on a much larger scale, to the dinner you were invited to. All our relatives came, like I said, as well as our friends. The dinner was potluck, but my grandma always made the *bimuelos*. Everyone would bring their favorites, and somehow, although no one sat and organized anything, we always ended up with the right number of dishes."

"So, no three pots of brisket and zero vegetables?"

Carrie laughed. "Nope. The celebration was always noisy, especially because we made sure to invite people we'd fought with during the year so we could make amends."

Arlo sat back. Would Isaac have invited him to a *merenda*? Would he have attended? Gosh, he hoped so.

"Wow."

Nodding, Carrie continued, "As the sun set, my grandpa would light our family menorah, everyone would eat dinner, and it was just a wonderful time."

"That's a great tradition. You should do that here," he said.

"How exactly?"

"I don't know," Arlo confessed. "But I'd certainly come."

"Anything for *bimuelos*," she teased. "By the way, this is delicious."

"And you made fun of me for not barbecuing."

"Okay, maybe I was wrong." She looked around the room. "Your home is beautiful, by the way. I didn't know people lived along the lake on this side."

"Thank you. My mom really lucked out when she purchased this spread. The former owners built the houses my sisters and brothers and I live in, and when we saw the views of the lake, we were hooked." He laughed. "Funny thing, we were told they were log cabins." He turned in a circle. "I don't know about you, but when I picture a log cabin, this is not what comes to mind."

All of the "log cabins" were huge A-frames with decks and huge windows overlooking the lake. The only thing "log" about them was the wood they were made of.

Carrie nodded. "No, me neither. But if the rest of them are anything like yours, they're stunning."

"Thanks. The lines are similar, but there are differences in style and decorating, especially as we've made ourselves at home."

"What about your mom?" Carrie asked. "You said she lives on the ranch, too?"

"Yes, that's right. Plus, she owns the Fortune Castle, which she's renovating and turning into a hotel and spa."

Carrie's eyes widened. "Wow."

Arlo nodded. "It's a crazy story," he said. "Maybe Randi mentioned it to you?"

Carrie nodded. "Yeah, she said something about your family inheriting the castle."

He toyed with his napkin. "My mom discovered she was the secret illegitimate granddaughter of Wendell Fortune. Apparently, the woman who raised her, the one I've always thought was my grandmother, was actually a babysitter hired to take care of my mom for a brief time while her real mother and father went off to elope." He took a long swallow of his beer before continuing. "But her parents died in the Chatelaine mine disaster in 1965, and the babysitter—Gertie Wilson—thought she'd been abandoned and raised her as her own. My grandmother left the truth in a letter that my mom opened after Gertie passed away, and she ended up meeting Wendell right before he died. He left the entire ranch and castle to my mom and now she's fixing it up."

"Oh, my, that *is* quite a story." She met his eyes. "And turning the castle into a hotel sounds like quite an endeavor."

"It is, but she is doing an amazing job with it," he told her proudly. "She goes back and forth between the two places a lot while overseeing the renovations but is currently residing in the main house on the other side of the ranch property. Actually, we all live here, which makes our jobs much easier."

"I'll bet it does," she said. "I envy you living so close to your family."

Sympathy filled Arlo. Carrie and Aviva were all alone here. He wanted to cheer her up. Actually, he wanted to take her in his arms and reassure her that she wasn't alone, but he suspected she'd pull away. He needed a distraction.

"Would you like a tour?"

Carrie looked around the kitchen, which was separated from the adjoining dining area by a huge marble island. "If the rest of your home is as impressive as this, yes please!"

"Yes pwese, yes pwese!" Aviva clapped her hands, making Arlo laugh.

"I'm glad you like it. Come with me." He led the two of them from the kitchen to his sunken living room. The huge fireplace, which he'd lit earlier, was framed by the same slate as the backsplash, stretched almost to the ceiling, with a black marble hearth and mantle.

Carrie paused in the middle of the room and sighed.

To their right, facing the lake at the back of the house,

were floor-to-ceiling windows, which followed the peak roofline. Although long past sunset now, his backyard was illuminated by lanterns, as was the dock on which they'd stood earlier. With the full moon reflecting off the water, it was brighter than normal. As usual, Arlo was stunned by the view as well.

He glanced at Carrie.

She was even more stunning. Her hair was pulled off her face with a clip, her sweater hugged her curves, and her jeans…well, they hugged her, too. The look of wonder softened her facial features.

"I don't think I'd ever get tired of this view," she whispered.

"Me, neither."

He responded without thinking, but when she glanced at him, a puzzled look on her face, he swallowed. "I mean, I don't."

"Do your siblings have a lake view, too?"

"They do, although we're all spread out with about thirty acres each. Still, if you look over there—" he stood behind her, one hand on her shoulder, the other pointing in the distance "—or there, you might be able to see their lights."

While she searched the shoreline, he enjoyed being close to her. Since he was tall, the top of her head reached his chin. Holding her like this was almost an embrace.

"Oh, yeah," she said. "I can see them over there." And then she shifted her posture, enough to add space between them, and the moment was lost.

"You'll have to come back in the daytime so I can show you the outside and the ranch itself. Plus, that way, Aviva can see the animals at the petting zoo. We have ducks and pigs and some baby chicks. My sister Jade runs it. She used to have a lamb in the zoo, but he got stressed, so she moved him into the barn with a goat for company."

Aviva's face brightened, and he held up his hand for a high five.

"We'd love to," Carrie said.

"Then it's a date." As soon as the words left his mouth, he froze. His blood rushed in his ears. He hadn't meant it the way it sounded…but at the same time, a date with Carrie, well, he wanted nothing more.

And yet the look on her face told him she wasn't ready.

Shoot, had he messed everything up?

"We'll have to put it on the calendar, so we don't get distracted by everything else we have to do," he said, the words sounding odd to his own ears.

But her relief was palpable.

"That would be fun," she agreed, giving Aviva a squeeze. "We'd like that, wouldn't we, Vivie?"

"I wike amals," she said. "Baa, baa, baa."

He tousled her hair, glad of the distraction, as Carrie laughed.

"So do I." He winked, looking at the toddler. Carrie hadn't refused the idea. It would take some time, but maybe she'd give him a chance.

The next day, while Aviva played with her toys and Arlo caulked some of the upstairs windows that were letting in drafts, Carrie worked at her computer. Her editors had loved the idea of a grief journey series and wanted to include such topics as the stages of grief, how to help someone going through the process and where to find help. Carrie put together a portfolio of articles and advice for distribution.

But all the while, thoughts of Arlo distracted her.

He'd been so kind last night, seeming to understand her discomfort and respond to it in exactly the right way.

And then he'd suggested the "date." She'd been taken aback at first, so he'd brushed it away as a time on the calendar, and now she didn't know what to do.

Her friend Emma was right. Carrie was attracted to him, there was no doubt, but the thought of focusing on a man when she was still grieving seemed wrong.

However, she couldn't deny the sparks of attraction that zinged between the two of them. From the tone of his raspy voice to the warmth of his flushed skin, she suspected— *no, knew*—he felt the same. And ordinarily, she'd act on it. In fact, a part of her wished he'd given her a little longer to come to terms with the idea before backpedaling.

But she also had Aviva to consider. The two-year-old was enamored with him, which should have lessened her concerns, but with so many changes going on in her young life, Carrie was hesitant to add anything else to the mix.

But oh, mama, he was hot. And the way he interacted with Aviva? Her ovaries convulsed every time. She wished Randi was here to talk to, but if she was, Carrie would be back in Albuquerque and most likely wouldn't be fighting this wild attraction for her brother-in-law's best friend.

Although she missed "home," Chatelaine was growing more appealing by the minute.

She sighed and opened her email. Her lawyer needed information for the adoption papers, and Carrie tried to focus on the task at hand.

"Earth to Carrie."

She jumped.

Arlo leaned forward. "I'm sorry," he said. "I didn't mean to scare you."

Swallowing, she tried to even out her breathing. "No, that's okay. I don't know why I'm so jittery."

Well, other than having a sexy man in her new home.

"Did you need something?" she asked.

"I'm running out to pick up a few things for your window. Need anything while I'm gone?"

You.

"Um, no, thanks, I'm good."

She breathed a sigh of relief, if only because she didn't have to worry about embarrassing herself in front of him.

Finishing her email in response to her lawyer's questions, she put away her laptop and made Aviva lunch.

"Okay, sweetie, nap time."

Aviva shook her head. "No nap."

"Okay, how about we read a story?"

"Yes!"

She followed Aviva over to the newly repaired bookcase in the living room and watched while her niece looked at all the books, finally pulling one out and handing it over to Carrie.

"Come, we'll read upstairs."

Slowly, they climbed the stairs together. Once in Aviva's room, Carrie sat in the maple rocker, removed Aviva's shoes and socks, and cuddled with her as they read the book she'd chosen. It was a story about a little girl and her *abuela* who hid her Jewish identity but incorporated it into her own customs at Christmastime. The subject was way above her niece's understanding, but Aviva loved the colorful pictures, and Carrie adapted the story to fit a two-year-old's mind. She kept her voice low and soothing, and thanks to the steady rocking of the chair, Aviva fell asleep before Carrie finished the book.

"That's an interesting story," Arlo whispered as he stood in the doorway.

This time, he hadn't scared her. He entered and helped her lift Aviva into her toddler bed, tucking her in, a tender expression on his face.

They stood over Aviva for a few minutes in silence before tiptoeing out of the room and shutting her door.

"Some of our ancestors came from Spain and had to hide who they were," Carrie said as they talked in the hallway. "They settled in this area, and most of the Jewish traditions were lost, but some still remained. The book is a little advanced for her, but I guess Randi wanted her to know about that part of our history."

"That's fascinating."

"Yes, they're called 'crypto-Jews' or 'Marrano Jews,'" Carrie explained. "Some are eager to embrace their Jewish heritage today, and others still don't."

"Wow, I never knew that."

Carrie smiled. "Did you get what you needed?"

He held up his paper bag. "Yup. But I'll have to finish tomorrow. I've got to get back to the ranch to talk to Nash about implementing some of his plans for the ranch, as well as Heath's new technology. I need an update about our bottom line, and well, other stuff." He looked sheepish. "I don't mean to bore you."

Carrie tried to hide the pit of disappointment in her stomach. Her sister's house—*her* house—wasn't big, but she'd grown accustomed to having Arlo around.

Liar, her conscience said. *You like having him around because you think he's sexy.*

"No problem," she said. "I really appreciate your time here. I'm sure you have a ton of your own work to do."

He shook his head, following her downstairs and grabbing his cowboy hat off the hook in the hallway.

"I enjoy doing this." He looked down at her, sincerity shining in his green eyes. "Like I said, it makes me feel good to help you out."

"Thank you." She watched him jog down her porch steps, shutting the door before he drove off in his car.

The next day, Arlo returned early in the morning. So early, Carrie was still in her T-shirt and pajama shorts, cooking pancakes.

"Knock, knock," he called, before letting himself inside. "Oh, man, I smell something good."

Carrie sucked in her stomach, hoping, somehow, he wouldn't notice her lack of bra. "Blueberry pancakes. Want some?"

"Does a bear—"

He paused, his face reddening, just as Aviva said, "Roar!"

Carrie burst into laughter, as did Arlo.

"Saved by the toddler," she said to him as he sat at the table next to Aviva. "Again."

"Sorry about that. Must have been overcome with hunger."

When he turned away, she reached for a sweater, before she served him three large pancakes and nodded toward the maple syrup. "Wouldn't want you to starve, then, would we?"

As the three of them ate breakfast, Carrie wondered what it would be like having breakfast with this man all the time. He easily joined in conversation with her and Aviva and helped the toddler with her food and drink.

Since Aviva had made the bear noises, he peppered their

meal with various animal sounds, adapting their game since they were sitting down to a meal.

"I swear, I'm going to gain a thousand pounds if you keep cooking for me," Arlo said as he finished.

"Well, then, you should probably avoid my house until Hanukkah is over. I'm planning to make lots of special foods."

His eyes lit up.

Was he always this appreciative of food, or was it her cooking? And did he just think she was a good cook, or was a budding attraction to her coloring his opinions?

And why do I care?

She wanted to shout at herself, to tell herself she was being a fool. But a small part of her liked the attention.

As Arlo went off to continue his work on her window, Carrie decided to cut herself a little slack. Yes, she was lonely. She grieved for her sister. But she also missed her life back in Albuquerque and her friends. Talking to them on the phone was harder to do the busier she became, and she missed them. And she definitely missed the Jewish community. Being with Arlo, however, softened those feelings, and being with someone who understood her grief was soothing. He was a wonderful man in so many ways, especially in his willingness to learn about her traditions.

It was time to stop analyzing every moment and just breathe.

Aviva ran over. "Cawwy, dwadel." She held out the red dreidel Arlo had given her.

Smiling, Carrie bent down. "You want to play dreidel, lovey?"

Aviva nodded.

"Okay, let's go find our pennies."

Taking her niece's hand, they walked into Isaac's office. Carrie swallowed in the doorway but pushed her way into the room. By now, she'd removed her brother-in-law's personal things, and while it still looked like an office, it could be anyone's. She was even considering transforming it into her own, but she wasn't sure.

Since Aviva liked playing the dreidel game so much, Carrie had begun collecting pennies and tossing them into a jar, which she kept on the desk. She pulled it closer.

"Here you go. How many do you think we need?"

Aviva reached her hand into the jar and pulled out a fistful. Some of them dropped on the floor. Carrie picked them up, took the remainder from Aviva's hand and nodded for her to take another handful.

"That's perfect," she said.

As they exited the room, Aviva cried, "Bye, Daddy."

Carrie's breath hitched. A lump formed in her throat. Tears pricked, but she didn't want to shed them. She didn't want Aviva to associate sadness whenever she mentioned Isaac or Randi. So, she swallowed and whispered, "Bye."

Back in the living room, she cleared her throat. "Are you ready?"

Aviva nodded.

Carrie spun the dreidel. It landed on *shin*.

"Shin, shin, put one in," Aviva cried, clapping.

"Good job!" Carrie said as she put another penny in the middle.

The next spin showed a *hay*. "Hay, take half," Carrie said and split the pile of pennies in half.

She spun again and landed on *nun*. "Nun means none." She frowned.

"None, none, none," Aviva cried.

"That's right."

One more spin, and this time, the dreidel landed on *gimel*. "Gimel is gimme all of them!" Carrie took the whole pile and laughed when Aviva clapped her hands.

Aviva's joy was infectious, especially when she grabbed all the pennies and slid them toward her. The child took to the game immediately.

She continued giggling as Carrie made a game of pretending to take Aviva's pennies, and Aviva tried to take Carrie's. She was having so much fun with the little girl, she didn't notice Arlo return until suddenly he was right next to them, smiling.

"What, no pennies for me?" he asked.

Aviva pushed herself up and gave Arlo all her pennies.

"Hey," Carrie cried. "What about me?"

Aviva shook her head no before hiding behind Arlo's leg. Carrie pretended to pout, but then the little girl peeked her head around and shouted, "Boo!"

Somehow, the game morphed into hide-and-seek, with Carrie and Arlo playing along.

Carrie wasn't sure what she enjoyed more—Aviva's contagious joy or Arlo joining in. Her senses spiked into high alert. Every time her arm brushed against Arlo's, or she exchanged a glance with him, time slowed, her skin prickled, her insides clenched.

Every. Time.

She didn't remember Hanukkah games being this interesting when she was a kid. Clearly, things were different in Texas.

Arlo had rushed through his paperwork in an effort to get back to Carrie and Aviva sooner. Maria, the ranch office assistant, had left him a pile of papers to sign. He'd had emails to read and return. And Ridge and Nash wanted to meet with him. But his attention wasn't on the ranch, it was on the two females playing Hanukkah games, and his attempts to clear off his desk failed.

While he'd signed all the documents, he'd read only half his emails and responded to none. He'd pushed Ridge and Nash off another day or two and flown out of the office and back to Carrie's house before anyone could argue with him. He expected at least one or two annoyed texts or phone calls, but he didn't care.

What he did care about was spending as much time as possible with Carrie and Aviva. Only with them did the all-consuming grief and guilt not press down upon him. Only with them did he smile and find himself forgetting his concerns. Only with them did he enjoy holiday preparation.

So yesterday, when he knocked on Carrie's door and no one answered, and when he opened the door to sounds of laughter, he couldn't help himself. He joined in.

And today?

Today he was sitting at her kitchen table watching her and Aviva make Hanukkah candles. Never mind that he should be outside fixing the mailbox that listed to the side. Never mind that the only candles he'd ever heard of being made from scratch were last made in colonial times. He sat at the table and stared at Aviva's chubby hands rolling beeswax into lumpy, misshapen, beautiful candles.

As one, he and Carrie praised the little girl's efforts and laughed at her rainbow-colored hands.

When they finished making the candles, Arlo helped clean up while Carrie left the room. He heard her steps retreat upstairs, but the running water while they washed their hands drowned out any other sound.

"All clean," he declared after inspecting each of Aviva's ten fingers.

"Aww cwean," she echoed, turning his hands over and scrunching up her face.

Carrie entered the kitchen, a pained look on her face.

"I found Randi's Hanukkah box," she said.

Arlo's chest ached. "You okay?"

She nodded, although her eyes looked misty.

"I was looking for their menorah."

She placed the box on the table and opened it. Arlo lifted Aviva into his arms so she could see—but not touch—the items.

Inside the box was a velvet case. Carrie opened it and ahhed.

"Look at this, Vivie." Her voice cracked, but she kept going. "This was Mommy and Daddy's menorah."

The nine-branched candelabra—one for each of the eight nights, and the helper candle—was a wave of rainbow-colored glass. Even with Aviva's misshapen candles, it would look beautiful when lit.

"Pwetty," she said, her mouth open. She reached her hand out to touch it, and Arlo guided it so she wouldn't break it.

"Let's see what else is in the box," Carrie suggested.

She pulled out several glass and ceramic dreidels. "Oh, these are beautiful," she said. "But they're just to look at, not to play with, okay? If we play with them, they'll break."

"I hold?" Aviva asked.

Arlo's pulse raced. This was asking for trouble. But Carrie was patient.

"Yes, but you need two hands."

Arlo put the toddler down, and Carrie cupped her hands

to show Aviva what to do. Aviva copied her. Then Carrie placed one of the dreidels in her hands.

Arlo smiled, but Aviva sat almost frozen, staring at the dreidel with a big smile.

"No more," Aviva said, after a few seconds.

Not knowing if the child was going to drop the dreidel or what, Arlo took it out of her hands and gave it to Carrie.

The smile she gave him warmed him. "Thanks."

"What else in there?" Aviva asked, pulling at the box flap and trying to stand on tiptoe.

"How about I lift you up?" Arlo asked, lifting her before she could answer him. Somehow, he suspected it was safer for her in his arms than near the box of fragile things.

"There are tablecloths and tea towels and some china trays with gelt on them." Carrie pulled them out and showed them to everyone. Nothing held Aviva's interest for long.

"Down pwese."

Arlo put Aviva down once again, and she ran to get her red dreidel. As Carrie placed the items around the house, Aviva added her toy dreidel from Arlo to the shelf where Carrie displayed the other dreidels.

"What a great idea, Vivie," Carrie said.

Aviva clapped her hands.

Arlo's chest swelled thinking how much the little girl liked the gift he'd given her.

"Just remember, we can't play with the other ones, only your red one."

"Onwy wed."

Carrie nodded. "That's right."

"Want help with the tablecloth?" Arlo asked.

He didn't know why that question popped out of his

mouth. Really, out of everything he could have asked, that was probably the most ridiculous. But here he was, having already spoken the words and now waiting for an answer.

"I'm going to wash them first."

And now he felt even more stupid, although he couldn't explain why. He stuffed his hands in his pockets. She didn't need him for this stuff. She *did* need him for repairs, and if he was smart, he'd get going on those things.

He pointed to the door. "Yeah, so I'm just going to get to work—"

Before Carrie had a chance to answer, he left the house, grabbing his tools and getting to work on the listing mailbox. Aviva's laughter echoed in his mind. *Gosh, that kid is smart.* He didn't know a lot about children, but he didn't think there were too many two-year-olds who understood so many things and spoke so well, even if she had a hard time pronouncing her *r*'s.

His chest tightened, thinking of all Isaac was missing. He remembered talking to him about his hopes and dreams for his baby when Randi was pregnant.

That man deserved to be a father. He would have loved every second of their Hanukkah celebrations.

He shook his head. Life wasn't fair. Then again, it wasn't fair his own father had possibly ruined two families—his own and Stevie's. Because now that Casper was dead, there was another child without a dad…

He pounded the nail into the wood so hard it cracked the rotting shelf. He swore under his breath, and turned to go find another piece to replace what he'd ruined. Inside the house, the smell of fried onions made his stomach rumble, and he followed his nose into the kitchen.

"What are you making?" he asked, hoping the awkwardness from before had disappeared.

"I'm making *keftes de prasa* and freezing them ahead of time for Hanukkah." Her cheeks reddened. "I should have asked you first if you'd like to try some. They're fried leek patties."

She looked at the pan sizzling on the stove. "I'll have another batch ready in a minute, if you want to wait."

She was always cooking, this one. "They smell delicious, but if I don't get work done, this house will fall down around your ears." And he'd never get over the guilt of failing his friend.

She nodded. "Well, they're here if you're hungry."

He was always hungry, but hunger didn't fix listing mailboxes. After he found another piece of wood, he returned outside and finished the repairs, determined not so shirk his responsibilities like his father had done. He straightened, looking between his truck and Carrie's house. Swallowing, he realized that's how he thought of this place now. If only he could be sure she'd stay.

He was about to go inside to say goodbye when she and Aviva appeared on the porch. Carrie put a tray with two mugs of hot chocolate and a sippy cup down on the table.

She nodded to the mailbox. "That looks so much better. Thank you. You know," she said, patting the rocker next to her, "Randi mentioned a mine to me. Do you know anything about it?"

It was like she'd read his mind—if she were interested in the town, maybe she wanted to remain here.

"Back in 1965, my great-uncles Elias and Edgar Fortune owned a secret gold mine, ignored warnings that it might be unstable and, as a result, caused a mine collapse that killed fifty-one people."

Carrie gasped. "Oh, my goodness. That's terrible."

Arlo nodded. "Yeah, the two brothers were pretty awful. They slunk out of town without taking any responsibility for the accident and supposedly died in a boating accident in Mexico. My great-grandfather, Wendell, was their older brother. And my grandmother was the fifty-first person killed in the mine."

"Oh, now I get it," Carrie said.

"Anyway, the mine didn't actually have any gold, only silver, but it's the source of our family wealth. Or it was. Now it's just a historical and tourist site."

"So that's why the town was originally founded?" Carrie asked.

"Yep. The castle belonged to my great-grandfather, who, as I'd mentioned, left it to my mom. Chatelaine Hills is where my family and some of the wealthier people settled as they arrived. You've probably seen the country club, right?"

She nodded.

"The townspeople are friendly and hardworking. Luckily, they don't seem to have a problem with my family and I, since they've been pretty welcoming to us since we arrived."

He wasn't big on gossip and hated to connect himself to the horrible relatives who had caused so much grief to so many people. Growing up with his father, he'd hated the idea of people talking about his family, and once he found out about his actual family history, he was even more careful. But he must have done something right because by the end of his conversation, Carrie was nodding.

"I can't wait to get to know these people now that you've painted such a vivid picture."

He tipped his head in acknowledgment, and inside he gave a mental cheer. If she wanted to meet people in town, she definitely wasn't planning on leaving anytime soon.

"You'll meet a lot of them if you join us for the holiday party," he said.

"Oh?"

"It's in ten days and held at the town hall. Practically everyone in town goes. There's music and holiday festivities. It's fun." He paused a moment. "You should come. With me."

There, he'd said it. He swallowed, wondering if she'd say no.

"I'd love to," she replied with a smile. "It sounds fun."

He took a drink of the warm liquid to compose himself. She wanted to go to the party. With him. Excitement made his body warm, his disappointment in his dad from earlier disappearing. If Carrie stayed, if he took her and Aviva to the festival, he'd have more opportunities to be involved in both of their lives. He could help Aviva get to know her father. His heart turned over.

She turned to him. "You've got something on your chin," she said.

He touched his face, but she shook her head. "No, here."

She dragged her finger across his jawline to his chin, and swiped a dollop of whipped cream. The contact sizzled. Before she pulled away, he reached for her hand and held on to her wrist. She froze, as did he. Around him, the silence thickened, except for the sound of his pulse pounding in his ears. Her lips parted and her chest rose and fell as her breathing increased. Her skin was soft beneath his. His fingertips pressed against her skittering pulse point.

He wanted to pull her close and feel her body against his. To nudge her hair away from her neck with his nose and press a kiss at her nape. To take the finger against his chin and bring it to his mouth and lick it.

But Aviva was nearby. They were seated on the front porch, where anyone could walk by and see them. And Carrie was still grieving.

Instead, he squeezed her wrist, a wordless promise of sorts. *More later if you're willing.* And he released her.

Her finger remained suspended near his chin for a few seconds, as if she didn't know what to do with it.

Or as if she wanted to stay close to him.

But then she lowered it to her side and turned away from him.

He waited for her to speak, watching her for any sign that she wanted him as much as he wanted her. His reward was the sight of her sides expanding and contracting, thanks to the snug fit of her shirt. He smiled to himself.

When she finally did speak, all traces of her desire were gone.

"Would you mind getting me several sheets of paper towels, please?"

He swallowed before doing what she said.

She took the towels from him and continued with what she was doing. And he made a decision.

"How about a break from it all?"

She looked at him, askance. "From what 'all'?"

"All the work you've been doing. Let's take tomorrow off, with Aviva, and go for a drive?"

"A drive where?"

"San Antonio."

Her eyes widened. "That's two hours away!"

"It'll be worth it, I promise."

She finished the last of the leek patties in silence, and he waited for her to say no thanks to his offer.

The idea, still formulating in his mind, had popped out of his mouth. But the more he thought about it, the more he wanted to get her away from here, with all the memories of her sister and brother-in-law, with all the pressures to pass down holiday traditions to her niece, and to just have a day of fun. With him.

"Okay," she said.

He was so caught up in his own thoughts, he almost missed her answer. But then he replayed the last few seconds and smiled. He'd have a whole day with her, away from the responsibilities and memories of this place.

And maybe a chance to make new ones.

Together.

Chapter Six

The following day, Carrie was up with the sun. She'd flown in and out of San Antonio before but hadn't explored it. She knew nothing about the city, nor did she know Arlo's plans. Without anything to go on, she dressed in jeans and a long-sleeved light blue top and tied a heavier sweater around her waist. She left her hair down and slipped on a pair of sneakers. Not leaving anything to chance, she'd packed a bag for Aviva with some toys and books and a variety of jackets and sweatshirts, pull ups and an extra pair of leggings.

"I wish he'd told me where we were going," she muttered to herself as she got breakfast ready. "Or that I'd thought to ask."

But at the time, she was reeling from being so close to him, from controlling her longing for him. All she'd wanted to do yesterday was pull his head forward and kiss him. Or wrap her arms around him and hold on tight. He'd grabbed her wrist, and they'd locked eyes, and she'd fallen deep into a well of desire. And then when he'd suggested spending the day together? Well, her brain and her heart and her body had thrown a party, and all she could do was nod and say yes. Luckily, she'd thought enough to make sure Aviva was included. But anything else useful would have to wait.

Ages had passed since she'd done something fun, something that wasn't a required task for either her sake or Aviva's. She didn't really care what they did today. She just hoped she was sufficiently prepared.

When Arlo showed up at ten, he came to her door, knocked and let himself inside. She'd grown to like that habit of his. It was starting to feel like he belonged here, which was weird, because it was she who was the outsider.

But with Arlo, she didn't *feel* like the outsider. She felt like she belonged.

"Are you ready?" he asked, entering the kitchen.

"Arwo!" Aviva cried. She ran over and hugged his leg, making Carrie smile. She was getting used to having him around, too.

"I'd be more ready if I knew what we were doing," she said. "But yes."

She pointed to the bags by the front door.

"I know it looks like we're moving, but toddlers need a lot of stuff."

Arlo laughed, swinging Aviva up into his arms and kissing her cheek before planting her on the ground again. "No worries, I have a big truck. Come on, kiddo, we're going for a ride."

"A wide? Yay!" Aviva jumped up and down.

They filled the two-hour trip to San Antonio with singing, pointing out the sights and laughter. Before long, they reached their destination.

"First stop, the San Antonio Zoo," Arlo said. "Who wants to see the animals?"

"Me!" Aviva yelled at the top of her lungs and bounced in her car seat.

Carrie smiled. "You sure know how to make her happy."

He flashed her a smile and squeezed her thigh, before

getting out of the truck and going around to Carrie's side to open the door. He was still smiling, and Carrie could have spent all day looking at him, his green eyes lit up, his dimples flashing. But Aviva was about to burst with excitement, so Carrie got the stroller while Arlo got her.

Once they had the child strapped in they entered the zoo.

"Which animal should we visit first?" Arlo asked.

"The zebwas!"

"Zebras coming up," Carrie said while Arlo pretended to be a zebra and galloped in front of Aviva.

When they reached the designated area, Arlo bent down to take Aviva out of the stroller and swung her up on his shoulders. His muscles bunched beneath his blue plaid shirt, and for a moment, Carrie wished she was in his arms. But the giggles and squeals from Aviva brought her back to reality. The little girl tapped Arlo's head with excitement, and Carrie exchanged a rueful glance with him.

"My niece is going to give you a headache," she said.

He shrugged, and they spent the next few minutes watching the black-and-white-striped creatures. Then it was on to the camels, the giraffes and the rhinos.

By now, Carrie was starving, and they stopped into Longnecks Bar & Grill, where they had a quick bite before resuming their walk.

"Okay," Arlo said, "we have time for two more animals. What should they be?"

"The wions," Aviva declared.

"The lions? And what about you, Aunt Carrie? What do you want to see?"

"She wants to see the monkeys," Aviva said.

"She does?" Arlo asked.

"I do?" Carrie echoed.

Aviva nodded.

Laughing, they walked to the lions, with Arlo roaring in Aviva's ear.

The toddler loved when the lions yawned, and she jumped when one roared a little too close to her. Carrie comforted her and they moved on to the monkeys, who were swung from the trees.

"I wike them," Aviva said, watching them in their enclosure.

"I like them, too," Carrie said. "Look how long their arms are."

Aviva tried to stretch her arms, and Carrie laughed. "I don't think that's going to work, Vivie."

"Alright, ready for our next adventure?" Arlo asked.

Carrie and Aviva nodded.

"Where are we going?" Carrie asked.

"Well, you can't visit San Antonio without visiting the Alamo," he announced. "Have you been?"

Carrie shook her head. "Nope."

"Excellent."

They drove to the tourist destination and visited the living history encampment. Although Aviva was young for the demonstrations, she watched, wide-eyed, as people walked around in costumes. She covered her ears at the musket demonstrations, and by the time they were halfway through, she'd fallen asleep in her stroller.

Carrie loved learning about the history of the site, and about the early years in Texas.

"I would not have wanted to get sick back then," she said, after listening to a demonstration about early medicine.

Arlo nodded in agreement. "Me, neither. Do you mind

if we go into the church? I reserved free tickets, but we don't have to use them."

"Of course not," Carrie said.

Arlo gave a sheepish smile. "Good. I wasn't sure if you'd want to..."

She paused, touched that he cared, but wanting to set the record straight. "Just because I don't worship in a church, doesn't mean I don't find them interesting," she said. "And this one has so much history attached to it. I wouldn't want to miss it." She pulled at his elbow. "But I do appreciate your checking with me."

They entered the hushed building. He was so considerate, Carrie thought as they wandered around inside. When he pushed the stroller and ushered Carrie around, she felt taken care of, for the first time in a long time. Maybe as part of her guide to healing-after-grief series, she should suggest finding a cute guy.

Scratch that—handsome, sexy rancher.

Who would have thought this nice Jewish girl from Albuquerque would fall for a cowboy?

She took a deep breath, for the first time in a while feeling relaxed and hopeful.

When they'd seen everything there was to see at the Alamo, Arlo led her outside. By now, Aviva was awake.

"Ready for our last stop?" he asked.

Carrie looked at Aviva, and they both said, "Yes."

This time, Arlo pointed them away from the car. "We'll walk this time."

Aviva swung her legs in the stroller while Carrie kept pace next to him. She looked at everything on their short walk, trying to take in as much of the trip as she could.

Arlo had been right. She'd needed to get away.

"Here we are," he said, pointing to the entrance. "The River Walk."

By now, the sun was beginning to set, and colorful lights filled the trees along both sides of the river. Holiday displays were everywhere, reflecting off the water and casting rainbow hues along the sidewalks and building facades.

"Wook, wook!" Aviva cried, pointing to the shimmering lights. "Pwetty!"

Aviva was right, Carrie thought. They *were* beautiful, actually. It was like walking through a multicolored fairyland.

Aromas of Texas barbecue, spices and sweets mingled, making her mouth water. Restaurants had installed space heaters for guests to sit outdoors. Colorful umbrellas covered tables, and small tour boats cruised the river, enabling tourists to float as well as walk. Strains of Christmas music projected from speakers and added to the festivities.

"This place is magical," Carrie murmured, turning to Arlo.

"I thought you'd like it," he said. "Although I'm sorry there aren't any Hanukkah decorations."

"I don't mind," she said. "I like experiencing your holiday like this."

Somehow, without her noticing at first, Arlo had taken her hand, and as they walked along the river, exploring shops, examining menus and admiring the holiday decorations, Carrie kept her hand in his, enjoying for the moment their time together. She didn't know what he intended by taking her hand. Was it an unconscious action, the first step of a plan, or merely the result of the festive mood on the River Walk?

She sneaked a glance at his profile. The lines and planes

of his face emphasized his confidence. At this moment, the signs of grief and guilt were gone. They were two people, spending the day together.

Carrie wanted more. The realization shocked her, but it was true. She wanted more than a day. When her sister had been killed, she'd dreaded a future without her. She still did. But in addition to that deep sadness, she finally wanted to see what her future held. And being with Arlo had helped her to see that her life hadn't ended when her sister died.

"Thank you," she whispered.

Arlo turned to her. "For what?"

Hope filled her chest, almost making her blurt out her feelings. But they were new, and she wanted to savor them herself for a little while longer.

"For today. For everything you're doing to help me. For your kindness to Aviva…" Her voice trailed off.

He squeezed her hand. "Thank you for letting me."

Now that she knew he was holding her hand on purpose, her joy increased. They continued along the river, showing Aviva the sights.

When the food aromas got to be too much, she pointed to a Mexican restaurant. "Want to stop?"

He nodded, and they settled at a table on the riverfront.

"Is it wrong of me to feel guilty for enjoying myself as much as I have today?" she asked him after the waitress took their order.

"I was actually thinking the same thing. I have so much on my mind, so much that's unsettled, but today? Today was just about perfect."

Carrie smiled. "Just about?"

He lifted one side of his mouth in a small grin.

The waitress arrived with drinks, interrupting the flow of conversation.

"I know Randi wouldn't want me to spend my days crying," Carrie said after the waitress left. "And everything has felt so overwhelming. But today, with you, was the first time I've felt myself in what feels like forever."

"I'm glad I could help," Arlo said. He reached for her hand across the table. "You've helped me, too. Somehow, being with you lightens the weight of my father's death, wondering about his other family, everything. I feel better equipped to confront things, and to learn to live without my best friend."

This time, she looked him straight on when their fingers touched. There was no mistake. His gaze was intense. Her desire was reflected in his eyes. A delicious thrill stole up the back of her spine at the realization he liked her as much as she liked him.

"I enjoy spending time with you," Arlo said. His smooth voice reminded her of the melodious sound of the cantor singing during Friday night Shabbat services—deep, rich and smooth. "I'd like to spend more time with you—free time—going forward."

"I'd like that, too."

He scooted his chair around, so they were on the same side of the table. Not releasing her hand, he cradled her face with his other hand, drew her close and kissed her.

His hand was warm, his lips firm, his kiss glorious. She closed her eyes, leaning into him, her skin flushing. His thumb made lazy circles against her cheek and sent shivers down her spine.

"Me, too, me, too," Aviva cried, puckering her lips.

With a laugh, they each kissed one of her cheeks. She gave them a huge smile.

"Well, this is going to be interesting," Arlo said, his eyes dancing.

"I can't wait," Carrie said with a wink.

Arlo left his office a few days later after another meeting with Heath to discuss his technology improvements. Numbers and technical terms jumbled in his head as he thought about Ridge's latest idea and how it would help the ranch succeed.

Running feet behind him made him pause, just as he was about to leave the building.

"Arlo, wait," Heath said. "Can I talk to you a minute? In private?"

Nodding, Arlo looked around before turning back to his office and shutting the door. He pointed to the chair across from his desk, and Heath sat, folding one leg over his knee and resting his ankle on it.

He steepled his fingers and focused on his sister's future husband. "What can I do for you?" The man was intelligent with a kind heart, perfect for Jade, and Arlo was willing to do whatever he needed.

"It's more of what I can do for you," Heath said.

"What do you mean?"

Heath expelled a breath. "We've been so focused on business, we haven't had a chance to talk much. And…" He rubbed the back of his neck, an awkward expression on his face. "You've been through a lot these past few months, especially after your friend died. I just wanted to check in with you. Jade and I are both worried about you."

Arlo's heart pounded and his face warmed. He didn't

know what to say. He opened and closed his mouth a couple of times, and then froze when Heath smiled.

"Yeah," Heath admitted, "it's a little weird coming at you out of the blue when we don't know each other well." His gaze sharpened. "But I know what it's like to lose people you love and to have the foundation shift beneath you. I know you've got lots of people to talk to, but I guess I just wanted to offer myself as one of those people if you need it."

Silence built in the room, until Arlo finally found his voice. "You've no idea how much your concern means to me," he said. "Not that I was ever concerned, but I couldn't have picked a better guy for Jade if I went looking for her match myself."

Heath's posture softened. "Thank you."

"No, thank you. You're right, it's been tough these past few months, and I've had a lot on my mind. It's nice to know you're here for me."

"Anything you want to get off your chest?"

He studied the man across his desk. If anyone would listen without judgment, it was him.

"I don't know, to be honest. I've found out something about our dad, and the secret is killing me. I don't want to make the rest of family feel even worse than they do, but I'm not sure how to handle it." He huffed. "I'm sorry for being so vague, but since you're with my sister, I don't want to put you in an awkward position, either."

Heath pinned him with a sharp gaze. "I appreciate that. You've all had complicated relationships with Casper, I get it. But there's no reason for you to suffer in silence, either. The thing I admire most about you Fortunes is you stick together. It's up to you whether or not you tell them what you've found out, but don't for a minute think they can't handle it or that you have to shoulder the burden yourself. You Fortunes are strong, a lot stronger than you think."

Heath was right. They were strong. Some of the burden that weighed him down, lifted.

He rose, as did Heath, and the two men hugged quickly, slapping each other on the back.

"Thanks, I appreciate it," Arlo said. "Really."

With a tip of his hat, Heath left.

Arlo was still ruminating on Heath's advice when his phone rang. He smiled when he saw the screen.

"Hey, Carrie."

"Hey, any chance you were planning to come over today?"

They'd been talking on the phone nightly before they went to sleep, and of course, during the day when he was working on her house, but he hadn't been there for a day or so.

"Why, do you need me?" Oh, the loaded words. He missed her, and honestly, *he* needed *her*, but he also had a job on the ranch he couldn't ignore.

"It's fine. I can do it myself."

"Wait, what's going on?"

He was on his way back to his house, and he sat in his golf cart, ready to drive it the short distance to his home.

"It's not a big deal. I didn't mean to bother you. I have to go to the lawyer's office regarding the adoption papers—"

"Whoa, that's a huge deal!"

Carrie huffed. "Well, yes, it is. I just meant I can bring Aviva with me. I don't want to take you away from working."

"What time is your appointment?"

"One o'clock. But, Arlo, if you have work on the ranch…"

He quickly figured out his day in his head. "Let me

clear up some things now, and I'll come to you by twelve thirty. Okay?"

"Are you sure?"

"Carrie, there's no one I'd rather spend time with than you or Aviva." He meant it.

"Thank you."

His pulse raced with the anticipation of seeing Carrie later, and an idea formed. Driving into town, he stopped at GreatStore, compiling a list in his head of the items he needed. On his way out, he bumped into his sister, Dahlia.

"Hey, there," he said, giving her a hug. "What are you doing in town?"

"I needed a few groceries. Feel like stopping for a quick cup of coffee?"

He looked at his watch. He had a little time before Carrie needed him.

"Sure."

They walked into the diner and grabbed a seat at the back. After fixing their coffees, Dahlia took a sip, while Arlo contemplated the advice Heath had given him. Should he talk over his dilemma with his sister? She'd been close to their dad. Maybe she'd have some insight.

"So how are you and Carrie getting along?" she asked.

He smiled. "I'm seeing her later. And Aviva." He filled her in on the adoption status.

Dahlia's face softened. "You're really attached to that little girl."

And her mother.

"Yeah. I am. She makes me feel closer to Isaac."

Dahlia reached into her bag and pulled out a sheaf of paper. "Do you think Carrie would mind if I made Aviva a blanket to celebrate Aviva's adoption?"

"I think she'd love it."

Dahlia smiled. "Good. I saw this pattern and thought it would be adorable."

He nodded. "Hey, how are you doing with Dad's death? I haven't checked in with you in a while, and I should have."

She stiffened before taking a deep breath. "I miss him. I know I'm probably the only one—"

"No, no matter our feelings for the man, we're all grieving. We just do it differently."

Heath might have been right about not shouldering all the responsibility, but Arlo wasn't sure Dahlia was the best person to tell his suspicions about their dad's second family.

That being said, as he said, everyone dealt with grief in their own way—his siblings, himself, Carrie. He'd do well to remember that, and maybe give everyone, including himself, some slack.

A few hours later, he knocked on her door, shopping bag in hand.

"Hi," Carrie said as she opened the door. "What's in the bag?"

He walked with her into the kitchen.

"I had an idea."

"Uh-oh."

He nudged her. "Go sign your papers."

"I have a couple minutes. Tell me about your idea."

For some reason, he was self-conscious. Part of him wished she hadn't noticed the bag, and that he could surprise her with his efforts when she returned.

With a sigh, he pulled out candy molds and handed them to Carrie. Her features softened as she looked at them.

"Dreidels and menorahs and coins. You're going to make gelt?"

He nodded. "I thought Aviva would have fun. We'll melt chocolate in the microwave and pour it into the molds. They'll refrigerate, and then she can have them for Hanukkah."

Carrie dropped the mold on the counter and hugged him tight. Then, she kissed him.

Man, if she was going to kiss him every time he had an idea, he'd ensure he turned into Albert Freakin' Einstein.

Her kisses were sweet and tender, but with a promise of more. His senses exploded as he tasted her sweetness, tangled his tongue with hers, and let the softness of her lips carry him away. She massaged his shoulders as she deepened the kiss, and his thoughts floated away. He grasped her waist, wanting more. He groaned as she stepped back.

"That's such a nice idea!" Sighing softly, she gazed up at him. "I have to go. I should be back in an hour or two. Thank you for all of this." She said goodbye to Aviva and left.

"Okay, kiddo, let's make chocolate!"

For the next hour, he helped Aviva make gelt. Or rather, he helped her make a mess. The gelt was a byproduct. But boy did he have fun. The two of them laughed and poured and melted and laughed some more. They were just cleaning up—seriously, two-year-olds could get chocolate in the weirdest places—when Carrie returned from town.

"Oh, my," she said as she walked into the kitchen.

Discarding her bag and her coat, she stood in the doorway and shook her head. "Any chance any chocolate ended up in the molds?"

Arlo walked to the refrigerator and pulled out a tray. "Ta-da!"

"Ta-da!" Aviva repeated.

He cracked the molds and turned the candies onto a dish.

"Wow," Carrie said. "I see dreidels, and a menorah or two, and some coins." She smiled. "Nice job, guys."

Aviva frowned. "I not a guy. I a girl!"

Arlo burst out laughing. "Yes, you are, sweets."

He turned to Carrie. "How'd your meeting go?"

"Really well. We have to go back in a few days—both of us—and appear before the judge, and then we're set."

"Congratulations. That's wonderful." Arlo's chest filled with happiness for them, but Carrie had a pensive look on her face. "Is there a problem?"

She shook her head. "No, it's just the final adoption makes it all real. I mean, I know it is, but it really hits home that there's no chance that my fantasy of Randi and Isaac showing up and saying, 'Surprise,' will happen. It's more final, even, than their funeral."

He put an arm around her, pulling her against him. She buried her face in his shoulder, and he held her while she breathed. Running a hand up and down her back, he warmed at her coming to him for comfort. She fit perfectly against him, and he was prepared to spend the rest of the day holding her if that's what she needed. But after a few moments, she pulled away. He brushed her hair away from her face and cupped her cheek.

"Do you want me to go with you? It's a big deal, and I could give you moral support."

She shook her head, her eyes bright. "No, I think it's

something I have to do alone." She expelled a large breath. "But thanks for today."

"Don't thank me until you're satisfied with the cleanliness of your kitchen. I had no idea chocolate could get in so many places."

"Oy." She laughed. "I appreciate the attempt, though. You should probably get back to work?"

He didn't want to. He wanted to remain here, with this beautiful woman and this amazing child. They filled him with hope and light, something he'd lacked recently. But he had work to do for Ridge, and he couldn't postpone it any longer.

"Call me later?" he asked as he put his Stetson on his head and his hand on the front door.

"Of course."

Carrie stood at the top of the town hall stairs a few days later. The building was a one-story adobe brick building with a weathered red roof. The cool wind made her shiver in her dress and heels. Aviva's nose was red from the cold.

Aviva. Her daughter.

She longed to have someone to share this momentous occasion with…like Arlo. But she'd been right when she refused his company. No matter how alone she felt, she had to do this by herself. Eventually she would be leaving Chatelaine and returning to Albuquerque. She couldn't always rely on Arlo.

She tipped her head back and closed her eyes, letting the wind ruffle her hair. The adoption was final, and Aviva was hers.

She knelt before the stroller. Aviva clutched the bear the judge had given her. "I promise to do the best I can," she said to the little girl. She looked up at the sky and mouthed *I promise* as well.

"My beaw," Aviva cried.

"What are you going to name it?"

"Beawy."

Carrie laughed. "That's a wonderful name. Welcome to the family, Beary."

Despite the chill in the air, Carrie was in no hurry to go home. The town hall was across the street from the GreatStore and Harv's New BBQ. She hadn't checked out their Texas barbecue yet, although everyone raved about it. Still, she wasn't hungry right now. Maybe she'd take Aviva to Remi's Reads, the local bookstore. As she stood on the stairs, trying to figure out which of her errands she should do, a woman walked up the stairs holding a stack of papers in her hand. She stopped in front of Carrie.

"Hi, do you know about the Chatelaine Holiday Celebration?" She handed Carrie a flyer.

Carrie skimmed it. "This sounds like fun. We'll be sure to come." She sighed.

The woman, even though she'd never met Carrie before, looked concerned. "Is there anything I can help you with?"

She was a little taken aback. This woman didn't know her. "It's nothing. I'm just being dramatic."

Leaning in, the woman whispered, "That's okay, sometimes it's necessary. Happens to me all the time."

Looking at the woman, approximately the same age as herself, with her hair in a ponytail, her face devoid of makeup, and wearing practical jeans, a gray turtleneck and a puffy vest, along with the requisite cowboy boots, somehow, Carrie doubted her statement. Still, it was nice of her to try to make her feel better.

"Are you sure I can't do anything for you?" she asked again. "By the way, I'm Rita. I'm on the committee."

"Hi, I'm Carrie Kaplan, and this is Aviva, my daughter." Carrie swallowed. It was the first time she'd said those words. It felt weird, but right, yet somehow still filled her with more emotions than she could process. Certainly nothing she would express here.

Recognition followed by sorrow crossed Rita face. "Oh, you're Isaac Abelman's sister-in-law. I was a good friend of Randi's. I'm so sorry for your loss."

Swallowing, Carrie nodded. "Thank you."

"She was such a sweetheart. Are you sure I can't help you with anything?"

"It's not a big deal. I was just hoping there might be something having to do with Hanukkah at the holiday celebration. I'm trying to teach my ni—I mean my daughter—about her heritage." *And feeling very alone.*

Rita's eyes widened, "Oh, my word, that's right, you're Jewish. We're having a bake sale to raise money for the poor in our community. We'd love it if you brought some Hanukkah baked goods. And I'm sure we can find some Hanukkah music to add to our playlist. In fact, I'll put that on my to-do list right now."

Carrie smiled, touched by the automatic inclusion. "I'd love to bake some treats. Thank you!"

"You're welcome." Rita looked her up and down. "You know, if you ever want to grab a quick bite, give me a call." Before Carrie could say anything, Rita wrote her number on one of the fliers and handed it to her, before waving and heading up the stairs into the town hall.

Carrie folded the paper and put it in her diaper bag. Not

yet wanting to return home, she wandered to the Great-Store, where she browsed among the aisles.

An elderly woman sat at the entrance of the store, greeting customers like old friends as they entered.

"Welcome to GreatStore," she said. "My name is Doris. Hello, little one, I love your bear!"

Aviva hugged the bear to her chest and smiled as Carrie greeted the friendly woman and continued walking. A manager, whose name tag read Paul Scott, nodded to her as she passed, and suggested she and Aviva check out the store's new photo studio. That sounded like a fun activity, and Carrie headed toward it.

"Hi, I'm Alana. Are you interested in getting your photos taken?"

Carrie looked at the woman who appeared to be close to her age. "I'd love to. The adoption just came through for us, and I'd like something special to commemorate it."

Alana's eyes brightened. "Oh, my goodness, congratulations! Come on over and we can pick a background for the two of you."

Carrie pushed the stroller over and looked at the options for a photo shoot. There were lots of Christmas decorations and plenty of options to turn the photos into a Christmas card.

"I don't suppose you have anything with a blue background?"

Alana nodded and showed her a dark blue drape with silver snowflakes. Since Carrie and Aviva were both wearing shades of pink, it was perfect.

In no time at all, Alana had taken several shots of Carrie and Aviva together, as well as several with the toddler holding her bear.

"These look great," Alana said. She handed Carrie a ticket. "Come back next week to pick them up. And congratulations, again!"

Ready to go home, Carrie headed back toward the entrance of the store. A middle-aged woman waved to Aviva and told her how much she liked her bear. And multiple salespeople said hello, offered her assistance and talked about the weather with her. She kind of liked the familiarity. Some of her earlier loneliness lessened. And aware that Aviva was always listening, Carrie made sure to carry on friendly conversations and be extra polite.

There were a lot of things to be aware of when you were a mother.

A mother. She was a mother.

Waves of joy and guilt crashed against each other, taking Carrie's breath away. Spots floated before her eyes. Her knees shook, and she leaned against a shelf. Eyes closed, she tried to get ahold of herself.

"Cawwy? Cawwy?"

Aviva's voice called through the fog.

"It's okay, Vivie. I just need a minute."

She needed more than a minute. She needed her old life back, her sister and brother-in-law...and Arlo.

Her breath hitched at the thought of him. Why hadn't she let him join her today? She wished with everything she had that he was here now.

"Ma'am, are you alright?" A young salesman looked at her, worry crossing his face.

"I...I'm fine." Her face heated. She hated making a scene. "I just need to catch my breath."

He spoke into his radio, but she didn't pay attention to what he said. Instead, she focused on calming herself down. But tears had started to fall. She tipped her head, hoping no one would see them. She was falling apart in the middle of the GreatStore in a small town where everyone would see and hear.

"Oh, honey, come with me." A woman's twang sounded close to her ear. "Let's get you out of here, okay? Winston, go open the office door. This woman needs to sit a spell."

"Thank you," Carrie whispered.

The woman patted her back as she led her into the back.

"You just sit right here and take as long as you need to get ahold of yourself. I'll be right back."

"Cawwy, why you cwy?"

She tried to wipe her face, but the tears wouldn't stop falling. Sobs built up in her chest, and she was afraid to speak for fear of scaring Aviva. So she took her hand and squeezed.

"Here you go," the woman said. She'd returned with a glass of water. "And I think the little one needs a c-o-o-k-i-e?"

Overcome by the kindness, all Carrie could do was nod.

"Sometimes the world gets to us and we just have to let it all go. Especially we women, who have to manage everything."

The older woman's wise words penetrated Carrie's grief. She needed to get ahold of herself. Just a few more moments and then she'd take Aviva and somehow get themselves out of the store with the minimum of embarrassment and go home, where she could cry in solitude.

They sat in silence, punctuated by Carrie's sniffles with her eyes closed and her head in her hands, until heavy footsteps sounded in the background and there was a knock on the door.

The chair legs scraped against the linoleum floor as the

woman rose from her seat next to Carrie. Muffled voices sounded, and then, the voice she'd longed for.

"Carrie?" Arlo's low voice made her open her eyes. "I hear you're having a rough time."

Before she could react to his sudden appearance or to ask how he knew, he took her in his arms. His warmth and strength surrounded her, held her together as she fell apart.

He pressed his lips to the top of her head and rubbed her back as he comforted her. His presence loosened the tight hold she'd kept on her emotions and sobs wracked her body. She gripped his shirt, and he tucked her against him, letting her burrow and soak his shirt without complaint.

After an endless amount of time, the tears stopped. Her breaths stuttered as she tried to calm herself, embarrassment returning. But still he held her, like it was the most natural thing in the world. Like needing him was okay.

When she finally pulled away, he looked into her eyes and brushed the hair out of her face.

"Hey," he whispered.

"Hey."

She looked around, fear knotting her chest. "Where's Aviva?"

"Myra took her to get a drink."

"Oh, no."

"It's okay. She's grandma to about sixteen kids at this point. I'll get Aviva when we leave. It's perfectly safe, I promise."

"Thank you." She crumpled again. "Look at me. I can't be a m-m-mother."

He gripped her hands. "Why not?"

"I'm not supposed to…be one now. I'm supposed to be

an…aunt. Randi is her mother." Her breath chopped. "I can't replace her."

He drew her to him once again. She shuddered in his arms. "I can't do this. I don't want to do this." She hit his shoulder with her fist, and he hugged her tighter. "I love her…more than anything. But it's not supposed to be…me."

"But how lucky is she that you're there to step in?" Arlo's voice whispered across the back of her neck.

She shook her head. "I'm going to…mess this up."

He took her by her upper arms and held her out in front of him. Staring into her eyes, he waited until she met his gaze. "You're an amazing woman. Of course, you're going to mess it up, lots of times probably, but you're not alone. There are so many of us who are here to help. Including me."

"I feel so alone." *And I shouldn't need so much help.*

He shook his head. "I know. But you're not. I promise. Look how everybody helped when they saw you having a tough time."

The band around Carrie's chest loosened. "I made a great impression as the crazy lady in the GreatStore."

Arlo smiled. "Nah, there've been others way worse than you." His expression grew serious. "I know it's overwhelming, but you're *not* alone. And I'd be honored if you'd allow me to help you."

She took a shaky breath and nodded.

"Think you're ready to go home?"

The thought of walking back through the store to her car filled her with embarrassment. It was one thing to cry in front of Arlo, which for some reason didn't bother her at all. It was something else to have to face the entire town of strangers. She closed her eyes.

"How crowded is it?" she asked.

"Doesn't matter. My truck is parked back here, and I have a car seat for Aviva." He pointed to the door next to them. "No one will see a thing."

Relief flooded through her.

He handed her a couple of tissues, and she blew her nose. When she nodded, he helped her up and walked her to his truck. "Wait here," he said, before disappearing back into the store.

She leaned her head against the headrest, shutting her eyes. She hadn't expected to fall apart. Today was supposed to be a good day. But somehow, as excited as she was to have the adoption finalized, the reality had hit her, and she hadn't been able to stop it. Even thinking about it now made her wobbly.

Arlo returned to the truck with Aviva.

"Wook what I got," she said, holding out a rainbow sprinkle cookie the size of her head.

"Oh, my goodness, that's huge."

Aviva nodded and gave a crumbly grin.

"Someone also got a lollipop and a toy horse," Arlo said.

Carrie's eyes widened. She'd have to thank the woman… What was her name? Myra. She'd have to thank Myra later. Never mind the incredible sugar high.

"You're one lucky girl."

"You feel better?" Aviva asked.

Carrie's heart beat hard in her chest. "Yes, sweetie." Guilt burned through her. While she understood the child hadn't known what was happening, she did know Carrie was sad.

Back at her house, Arlo got Aviva settled while Carrie

went to her room to sort out her face. She was a red mess. Her mascara was almost completely gone.

Great, just great.

That meant it was probably all over Arlo's shirt. That would teach her to move back to waterproof mascara permanently. She'd thought a month after Randi died was safe.

Nothing was going to be safe again.

She cleaned herself up as best she could and then sat on the edge of her bed, shoulders slumped. This was supposed to be a joyous occasion. How was she supposed to celebrate when the entire reason she'd gotten to this point was the death of her sister?

A soft rap on the door made her look up. Arlo stood in the doorway of her bedroom. His blond hair was finger combed. And his shirt, as she suspected, had tear stains and mascara smears. He held a glass of water.

"May I come in?"

She nodded. "I'm sorry about your shirt." Her voice was hoarse from crying.

He entered and handed her the water. Then he looked down at his chest and shrugged. "No biggie. Kind of adds character." The cold water soothed her parched throat. She placed the glass on the nightstand before looking at Arlo once again.

"You're very kind," she said.

He joined her on the bed.

"Maybe."

Turning toward her, he ran a hand through her hair and down the side of her neck.

This time, his touch wasn't as comforting as before. Not that it was bad. Oh, no. It was good. Her head and neck tingled at the contact, and she arched toward him.

His eyes were green, like emeralds. How had she never noticed their shade before?

"I like your lashes natural," he said, a glimmer of a smile on his lips.

"So does your shirt." Carrie touched the marks on the fabric, lingering as she felt the hard muscles of his chest. She started to move her hand away, but he clasped it against him.

They sat together for a few moments, the only sound their breathing. Then, very slowly, he leaned forward to kiss her. His lips met hers. Their gentle exploring made her yearn for more. He tasted like mint. He kept his hand on top of hers, but with his other hand, he cupped the back of her neck and brought her forward, so there was hardly any space between them and nowhere for her to go.

Which was a good thing because she didn't want to move. She wanted to know more about him—the texture of his skin, the slope of his shoulders. She ran her free hand through his short hair, the waves curling around her fingers, and then over his sculpted shoulders to his back.

He never stopped kissing her, and when she sighed against his mouth, he continued exploring with his tongue.

Carrie moaned, before pulling away. "Aviva," she said.

"Is napping," he answered.

With a smile, she pressed her lips against his. This time, with both hands free, she wrapped her arms around his waist.

He placed his hands on her hips, giving her freedom to move, but making sure she knew he wanted her to stay right here. And she had no desire to leave.

His shirt was soft from wear and untucked. She played with the hem of the cloth, and before she had time to think about her actions, she'd slipped her fingers beneath the shirt and against his warm skin.

He deepened his kiss, as if telling her he liked what she was doing.

Good.

Kissing sideways was giving her a crick in her neck and preventing her from savoring him as much as she wanted. She climbed onto his lap, and he smiled against her, a deep-throated growl expressing his pleasure.

All of her sorrow and embarrassment and bewilderment coalesced into desire. She wanted him, and she wanted to forget just for one minute how her life had changed.

Gripping her tighter, he fell back against the mattress, bringing her with him. Sprawled on top of him, their bodies pressed against each other, Carrie let all her cares drift away. Surrounded by his strong arms, possessed by his mouth, she wanted nothing else but to disappear. As he hardened beneath her, demonstrating his need for her, desire coiled.

"I want you," he whispered.

His eyes darkened with desire.

"I want you, too," she answered, barely willing to pull away long enough to speak.

He smiled, before rolling her to the side and lifting her shirt over her head. Exposed to the cool air in the room, her skin developed goose bumps, and he drew her to him once again, rubbing his palms over her back and arm.

"I want to see you undressed," she said as she lay on his chest, listening to his heart beat beneath her ear. The request increased his heartbeat, and he fumbled with the buttons on his shirt until he ripped the clothing off and flung it across the room.

His chest was muscular and tan, and she trailed her finger over it until he shuddered. She gave him a wicked grin before planting kisses all along his bare skin.

"Enough," he ground out, taking her by the upper arms and flipping her onto her back. "My turn."

He did to her what she'd done to him, and she marveled at how he'd remained on the bed. Beneath his touch, she arched and moaned, and that was just when he stroked her with his fingers. When he repeated the process with his mouth, she gasped. His kisses were hot and wet, and her body trembled with need. When she couldn't take his torture any longer, she pushed against him, once again, taking the upper hand.

As he lay back on the bed, a grin on his face, she pulled at the snap of his jeans and unzipped his fly before he had a chance to stop her. His grin turned to shock as she took him in her hands, running along the length of him. His skin was smooth and warm to the touch, yet beneath he was hard.

He stared at her, eyes glittering, until she leaned forward and kissed him.

"I want to see you naked," he rasped.

While she kept her hands on him, he sat up and removed her clothes. Finally, they were both naked. They paused, each drinking in the sight of the other.

"You're beautiful," he whispered.

They came together. His skin was rougher than hers, his muscles more defined. But they fit perfectly, and they quickly learned each other's rhythm. Before they got too carried away, Arlo paused and grabbed a condom from his jeans that were still partially on the bed.

Carrie took the foil packet from him and slid the condom on, enjoying how her touch unraveled him.

Finally, they were both ready. Carrie stared into his

eyes, drowning in their green depths. He discovered all her sensitive places with his hands and his breath—beneath her chin, under her left rib, above her right knee. Heady with sensation, she mapped his body with kisses, lingering at the notch in his collar bone and the indent of his right pelvic bone. Her skin was on fire, her nerves sending jolts of electricity throughout her limbs, until she didn't think she could take it anymore.

When she was just about to scream in a combination of frustration and need, he flipped her beneath him, supported himself on his straightened arms on either side of her and, with a nod from her, eased his way into her. Her body welcomed him, expanding around him but never completely losing the tension. He gritted his teeth as he pushed farther and farther, until finally they were as close as two people could be. Once again, Arlo asked her with only his eyes if she was ready, and when she nodded, he began to move. She followed him, adapting to his rhythm as if this wasn't their first time together, as if this wasn't a momentous, extraordinary event.

Carrie could barely hold on to a thought, but the "right-ness" of this moment and this person with her enveloped her. He was her safe harbor, her "yes, you can" when she was sure she couldn't. He was sexy and smart and fun. And he was hers, for the moment. As their bodies performed an age-old dance, she let herself go, matching his movements and straining as she got closer to her peak of desire. She grabbed hold of him and arched her back. As he drove into her one more time, she crested the wave, sparks dancing before her eyes, and she shouted her release. He thrust a couple more times before joining her as they both spiraled out of control. Minutes later, as their breathing eased and their sweat dried, he turned to her.

"You're amazing," he said.

She gave him a serene smile. "It was wonderful. Thank you."

He cradled her in his arms, and they lay peacefully, drifting in the hazy afterglow.

"Thank you for being there for me when I fell apart earlier," Carrie whispered.

He turned and caressed her cheek. "Always. You never have to thank me. And thank you for tearing me apart just now." He winked at her, and she elbowed him in the ribs.

"Oof," he said.

She laughed, turning on her side and draping a leg over him.

"Are you feeling better?" he asked.

"Now that I've elbowed you? Much."

Chuckling, he added, "You know what I mean."

"I do," she said. "And I am."

"Feel like celebrating Aviva's adoption later?"

Joy, the piece that had been missing from earlier in the day, filled her. "Yes, I'd like that."

"Great," he said, sitting up and swinging his legs over the bed. He began to dress.

Carrie eyed him, wondering why he was in such a hurry. "What are you doing?"

"I have things to get."

"Like what?" she asked.

He shook his head. "Things."

She rose and started to get out of bed. "Well, I have cooking to do if we're celebrating," she said, reaching for her shirt.

At that moment, Aviva cried out, and Carrie hurried up.

Arlo held out his hand. "No, you stay and relax. Aviva and I will take care of everything."

"Even the cooking?"

"*Especially* the cooking," he said. "Seriously, relax and take it easy."

He strode to her side of the bed, leaned down and kissed her. "We'll be back."

He turned to the door. "Coming, Aviva!"

Chapter Seven

Arlo swung the stroller around as he walked around the lake by his house. After a tumultuous day, Carrie needed rest more than ever. And he loved spending extra time with Aviva. They'd made shapes of the clouds, admired the different trees and wildflowers on the water's edge, and even collected a few rocks to bring back to Carrie.

"Hey, Arlo!"

Dahlia's voice pulled him up short, and he waved to his sister sitting on the back deck of her house. He turned the stroller her way and met her at the edge of her property.

"Morning," he said, bussing her cheek.

"Hey, cutie," Dahlia said, kneeling down next to the stroller.

Aviva was shy, but Dahlia soon got her to open up, and pretty soon his sister and Aviva were jabbering and laughing together.

Rising, Dahlia turned to him. "The blanket is almost done," she said. She nodded with her chin. "Just needs a red border, since clearly, that's a favorite."

Arlo laughed. "It is."

"I wove wed," Aviva said.

"I can see that," Dahlia said, pointing to the toddler's red shirt and red bow in her hair.

"She picked her outfit today," Arlo said.

Dahlia's eyebrows shot to the middle of her forehead. "Oh, really?"

Arlo's face heated. He'd just given away that he spent more time at Carrie's.

"I'm glad to see the two...three of you getting on so well."

He nodded. "I'm happy." His chest expanded. For the first time in a long time, he meant it.

Reaching toward him, Dahlia pulled him into a hug. "I'm so glad, little brother" she whispered in her ear. "So glad."

He pulled back, looking into her eyes, and hoped he wouldn't disappoint her when he found out the truth about their father. But for now, he'd take it.

Giving her a last squeeze, he said goodbye and continued on his way. They had a busy day, and it was time to get moving.

Back at Carrie's house later that afternoon. Turning off his truck, he released Aviva from her booster seat and gave her a small bag to carry to the door. Then he grabbed the rest of the bags and made his way to Carrie's front porch, where he somehow managed to get the front door open without dropping anything.

"Whoa, you guys have a ton of stuff," Carrie said, peeking among the bags in Arlo's arms. "I almost didn't recognize you. You're like bags with legs."

Aviva giggled her way toward the kitchen and put the bag on the floor. Arlo followed her, putting his bags, and then Aviva's, on the counter.

"We have a lot to celebrate, so we needed a lot of stuff.

Plus," he said, kissing Carrie, "two-year-olds don't exactly understand the term 'moderation.'"

"Neither do you, it appears," she said, nodding toward everything. "What in the world did you buy?"

"Wainbows!" Aviva cried.

"Rainbows?" Carrie swung Aviva up in her arms. "I love rainbows."

"Me, too," she said.

"That's a *lot* of rainbows," Carrie mused.

Arlo propped his hands on his hips. "Go sit in the living room, or go to work, or whatever. I've got this."

"I already worked while you were gone. I don't want to sit. There's nothing wrong with me. Let me help."

"Alright," Arlo relented. "How about you and Aviva put up decorations in the dining room?"

"That sounds fun." She smiled at the child, who was jumping up and down. "Wait, though. What are you going to be doing?"

"Something else. Now shoo."

Rolling her eyes, she took the bags he pointed out and left the room with Aviva. Their voices carried throughout the house as they decided what to decorate where. Now was his chance. Excitement raced through him. He opened his laptop, pulled up the website for the Chatelaine Bar & Grill and placed an order for home delivery with his cousin Damon. Adoption day was a big deal. His heart expanded as he thought about how much he'd grown to care about Carrie, and how special Aviva was. His pulse raced with the chance to share in the celebration. He wanted Carrie and Aviva to feel special. As great a cook as she was, he didn't want her having to do any food prep tonight. He looked at the time, figuring out when the delivery would arrive. Then he walked into the dining room.

"Looks great," he said.

Carrie was standing on a step stool, hanging red streamers—Aviva's choice—and signs saying Happy Day and Welcome. Aviva was holding the decorations out to her and wrapping herself up in them at the same time. All the little girl needed was some glitter, and she could be the centerpiece.

Which, when you thought about it, was true. Maybe if Carrie looked upon it as a way to celebrate Aviva, rather than emphasizing the awful thing that happened, she'd feel better. He'd have to find the right time to suggest it to her.

He paused. Was there a way for him to change his perspective when it came to his father and Stevie? He'd have to mull it over later. They were celebrating now.

"Thank you," Carrie said as she climbed down off the step stool. "Okay, Vivie, what's next?"

"This one," she said, holding out another sign.

"May I?" Arlo asked.

When Carrie nodded, he took some tape and attached the sign to the window. He turned and saw Carrie shaking out a rainbow tablecloth. Grabbing the other end, he helped her spread it on the table, while Aviva smoothed out the wrinkles—or made more, depending on your perspective. Finally, all that was left were the red balloons. He grabbed one from the bag and began to blow it up. Carrie joined in. The first balloon was Aviva's, and she chased after it, letting the adults finish their job alone.

Carrie looked around. "This is—"

"—very red?"

She laughed. "I was going to say festive, but you're not wrong."

He winked. "I suppose it could be worse."

"Yes, she could have chosen a glitter theme. I might have had to murder you."

"No glitter, gotcha." He pretended to take notes, and she laughed, which filled him with warmth. He was happy he'd been able to cheer her up.

"What do you think?" she asked. "Are we good with balloons?"

"That's up to you," he replied. "I think we are, but you're the boss."

"Actually, I think Aviva's the boss. Hey, Vivie, do we have enough balloons?"

The toddler scrambled over, still playing with the one they'd first given her. "Yes!" she cried. "I wike bawoons."

"I know you do, sweetie," Carrie said, scooping her up in her arms. "And this party is for you, so all these balloons are yours."

Aviva's eyes got big. "Yay!"

The doorbell rang, and Carrie turned to Arlo, a frown marring her smooth features. "Are we expecting someone?"

He kissed her cheek—Aviva was right there—and headed toward the door. "Don't worry. It's part of the surprise."

"Arlo, I'm not dressed for guests," Carrie protested, following him into the foyer.

He looked her up and down, his pulse quickening at the sight of her. She was wearing leggings and a sweatshirt with the neck enlarged so it hung off one shoulder. He wanted to lick it.

"You're dressed perfectly," he said. He opened the door and took the food bag from the delivery person, handing him a tip and shutting the door. "Besides, it's just dinner."

"You ordered food?"

His mouth dropped open. "You can't have a party without food! Do you want us to starve?"

Shaking her head, she followed him back to the kitchen. "God forbid."

"Good thing I'm in charge of food," he said.

"You seem to be in charge of everything."

Turning to her, he pulled her into his arms. "Anything you'd like me to change?"

She shook her head. "No, it's perfect."

"*I'm* perfect, you mean." He winked at her, and she kissed him.

It was a brief kiss, but it filled him up inside.

"At the risk of stoking your ego, yes," she said.

He whooped, making Aviva laugh. Carrie rolled her eyes, but he wasn't fooled. She liked the mischievous side of him. She was more relaxed than he'd ever seen her.

"Go sit down, and I'll bring out the food in a minute."

"That's silly," she said. "I can help."

"Nope, this party is for you as well. You and Aviva go sit down."

They disappeared through the doorway into the dining room, and he quickly got to work putting all the food on the serving trays he'd bought. He didn't want her to have to do any dishes afterward, and he wanted everything to look festive. One by one he brought everything to the table with a flourish—roasted root vegetables, boneless BBQ ribs, chili, fried potatoes and a salad. The Chatelaine Bar & Grill was one of the nicer restaurants in town, known for its delicious food, and he hoped Carrie would like the traditional Texas meal.

When everything was presented to his liking, he sat across from Carrie and Aviva. He poured red wine into his and Carrie's glasses and made sure Aviva had juice in her sippy cup before raising his tumbler in a toast.

"To the two of you. One, a strong and compassionate woman. The other, a smart and vibrant girl. Together, the two of you will make a formidable team and a wonderful family. Aviva is a very lucky little girl, and you are right where you belong."

Carrie's eyes welled, but she clinked her glass against his and Aviva's sippy cup and took a drink. Gosh, she was beautiful. He shouldn't be thinking that during such an emotionally charged moment, but sitting across from her, he couldn't help himself. And he was privileged to be here with the two of them on adoption day. She could have thanked him for his help and told him she wanted to be alone. But she'd let him stay.

How did he ever manage his days without her? The thought of filling them with work, as much as he enjoyed what he did, felt unimaginable, if Carrie and Aviva weren't there, too. He wanted to say something, to tell her how he was feeling, but he hesitated. She was overwhelmed. This day was about her and Aviva. No matter how badly he wanted to say something, he had to wait.

They ate their meal in a companionable silence, breaking it now and then to entertain or tease Aviva.

When they finished, he looked at the little girl's face and laughed. "I think she has more barbecue sauce on her face than was on the ribs," he said, chuckling.

Carrie looked at Aviva and joined in. "Oh, my, I'm not

even sure a bath can get you clean. Is that sauce in your hair?"

The child took her sticky, saucy hands and reached for her head. Realizing her mistake just a moment too soon, Carrie jumped. Arlo started to say something, but it was too late. The once blond curls were red and matted to her scalp.

"It is now," he said dryly.

"I don't suppose I could hose her down?"

He shook his head. "I wouldn't advise it. We need a photo of this."

Carrie's eyes lit up. "Oh, we do! And I'll have to show it to whomever she chooses to marry someday, too."

"Okay, but only after the vows. You don't want to scare anyone away."

"Aww, even with this face, no one will run away," Carrie said, reaching over and getting mere inches away from the messy toddler.

"How about we save dessert for after the bath?" Arlo suggested.

"There's dessert, too?"

"Of course. You can't have a celebration without dessert. It's against the rules."

Carrie shook her head. "You're like a child sometimes, you know that?"

He grinned. "That's why Aviva loves me, right?"

"I wuv you, Arwo. I wuv you, Cawwy."

"Aww, I love you, too, sweetheart," Carrie said. "Now, let's figure out how to get you into the tub without getting me saucy."

Arlo slipped around to the other side of the table to help and whispered in Carrie's ear, "But I like you saucy."

She swatted him away, laughing. Arlo removed Aviva's

tray and strap, while Carrie carried her with arms out-stretched into the bathroom. As he got the bath ready, she stripped the child of her clothes and deposited her gently into the warm water. Together, he and Carrie washed her until all traces of the barbecue sauce were gone. While Carrie dried her and got her into pajamas, he returned to the kitchen to clean up and prep dessert.

He and Aviva had stopped at the GreatStore's bakery while they were out and picked out a cake. Somehow, Aviva had kept its presence a secret, and now, he thrilled at the thought of the surprise.

He brought the cake out to the dining room just as Carrie and Aviva were sitting down.

"Cake!" Aviva cried, clapping her hands.

"Oh, that's so nice," Carrie said, reading the inscription on the top of the chocolate cake. "Happy Adoption Day!" She looked at Arlo. "Thank you."

"I hope it's appropriate," he said, suddenly nervous. What if she didn't like it? Or what if it was wrong in some way?

"It's perfect," she assured him. "And I know a prayer that I'm going to say. It's called the *Shehecheyanu*, and we say it on the first day of something new." She looked at Aviva and then back at him. "I don't know if it's the 'rule,' but I think it's appropriate."

Arlo listened as she recited the blessing to Aviva. The Hebrew words were foreign to him but had a musical qual-ity coming from Carrie. Even Aviva was enthralled…for a second. And then she wanted cake.

Carrie sliced pieces for everyone. "Oh, no, I'm going to have to bathe you again, aren't I?" she asked as she gave Aviva a piece.

"How about I feed her?" Arlo offered.

When she nodded, he scooted around to the toddler's side of the table and alternated between feeding himself and feeding Aviva, while Carrie ate her piece.

When they finished, Carrie cheered. "Yay, no mess. By the way, that cake was delicious. Where did you get it?"

"From the GreatStore. When in doubt, go there."

"Good to know."

They finished cleaning up after dinner and put Aviva to bed. Arlo didn't want to leave, but he didn't want to force Carrie to be with him if she wanted time alone.

"You've had an overwhelming day," he said when they left Aviva's room.

"It's been a lot," she agreed and turned to him. "But thanks to you, I got through it." She rose on tiptoe and kissed him.

Relief and desire flooded through him, and he pulled her close as he kissed her back. Pulling away, he searched her expression. "I don't want to overstay my welcome," he said. "So, if you want me to go, tell me."

She leaned against him, the top of her head against her chest. "I don't want you to go, but I think I need you to."

Now he was confused. "Why?"

"Because I need to know I can handle all this alone. You saved me today, but I have to save myself, too. So as much as I'd love you to stay here, I haven't really been by myself lately, and I think I need to be. In the silence, where all there is to do is think. Do you understand?"

He did, as much as he didn't want to. If he were honest with himself, he'd avoided spending time by himself so as not to think about his own issues. He respected her for her independence, as well as her acknowledgment of what she had to do. "I do. I don't like it, but for selfish reasons."

He kissed her again before grabbing his Stetson off the hook, followed by his jacket. "Call me if you need anything. Anything at all."

He left her, looking over his shoulder as he made his way back to his truck and over to his home. The large house was empty. *Too* empty. As he grabbed a beer from the fridge, he thought about how happy he'd been in Carrie's small home, with laughter and messy sauce and a happy occasion. Even with glitter and tears, he would have been happy.

He sighed. He'd done the right thing, not telling her how he felt. He still had his father and Stevie's past to figure out before he focused on his future. But he was going to have to do it soon.

As Carrie and Aviva pulled up to the town hall in Arlo's truck three days later, she gasped. Someone had decorated the town hall with rainbow-colored lights along the roofline. White lights wrapped around every fence post and tree in the vicinity. And two tractors on either side of the building sported *Happy Holidays* wreaths, and lights decorating them.

"Wow, this town goes all out for the Chatelaine holiday party," Carrie said, climbing out of the truck and unbuckling Aviva from her car seat. She stood next to the cab holding her daughter, transfixed by the sight. There was something about holiday lights that brought her joy, even if they weren't celebrating her holiday. It was the season.

Arlo came around to her side and put an arm around her. "Not bad."

She poked him in the ribs. "Don't tell me Mr. Grinch likes it," she teased.

His mood had lightened recently, and she was pretty sure he'd take her words for the joke she meant them.

"We'll see," he said. The corners of his mouth twitched, though, and a glimmer of joy shone in his eyes.

She'd take it.

They carried the platters of food she'd made for the party—sweet cheese pancakes, *bimuelos* with orange glaze, spinach patties, leek patties, fried pastry frills and chocolate gelt.

"I can't believe they asked you to make all of this," Arlo grumbled as he balanced the trays and navigated the door at the same time.

"They didn't," she said. "I couldn't sleep last night, so I cooked more than what I promised."

He eyed her over the pile of food but remained silent.

Inside the town hall, the holiday decorations continued. Lights outlined doorways, wreaths hung on doors, there were multiple decorated Christmas trees in the foyer, and the display case that usually highlighted Texas artifacts displayed a Hanukkah menorah, a Kwanzaa kinara and a snowman. Music piped in over speakers, and paper snowflakes hung from the ceiling.

To their right, tables covered in silver clothes displayed holiday foods, so Arlo and Carrie headed that way.

Carrie spotted the woman she'd seen on the steps a few days ago. "Hi, I don't know if you remember me, but I'm Carrie, and I offered to bring Hanukkah food."

Rita's eyes widened. "Of course, I remember you! Holy cow, you brought a lot!"

"I hope it's okay. There are so many tasty treats that I couldn't decide which to make."

"We will never turn down food," another woman said as she started moving other platters around to make more space. "By the way, I'm Shirley. It's nice to meet you."

Once the food was set, Carrie and Arlo and Aviva explored. The library sponsored a holiday story time in one of the meeting rooms. In another one, people could make and display holiday crafts. And in a third, there was a gingerbread house contest. Tables lined the walls of the room, and each table held a trio of different and elaborate gingerbread houses. Some were traditional and others were out-of-this-world creative. The three of them oohed and aahed at the gingerbread spaceship someone had created. Aviva clapped her hands at a gingerbread zoo, complete with candy animals. And the gingerbread ranch in the center of the room, with moving parts including a Santa popping out of a barn door, wowed them all. They spent some time at the story time, and Aviva listened to a story about Kwanzaa. In the craft room, they chose to make a menorah out of empty toilet paper rolls and colored tissue paper.

"See, there's the glitter," Arlo quipped.

"Thank goodness it's here and not at home," Carrie added as Aviva dumped a ton on her menorah. While the menorah dried, they wandered over to the gingerbread houses.

"These are so pretty," Carrie said.

"Look at this one." Arlo pointed. "It's like a mini ranch. I wonder who made it?"

Carrie searched for a name, but there was only a number. "I guess they want to maintain anonymity for voting," she mused.

After studying the rest of the houses, they returned to the foyer to taste some of the food. The sweet and savory scents combined to make Carrie's stomach growl. Grabbing plates, they filled them with a variety of foods, including some of what she had made.

Arlo's face showed pure bliss. "Oh my gosh," he said with his mouth full. "This is so good."

"Is my math whiz brother eating again?" A deep male voice sounded from behind Carrie's shoulder.

A smiling man—tall, lanky with dark brown eyes—and a woman with a baby stroller approached.

"Hi, I'm Ridge, Arlo's brother." He held out his hand and Carrie shook it.

The woman beside him had long, dark auburn hair, and her baby looked to be about seven months old.

"If Carrie cooked for you, you'd know to grab these while you can," Arlo said, punching his brother in the arm.

Carrie's face heated at the compliment.

"From the look on Hope's face, obviously, I have to try them," Ridge said. He reached over and took a bite of a leek patty from Hope's plate.

His eyes widened. "I see what you mean, bro. Carrie, these are wonderful."

Hope pulled her plate out of Ridge's reach. "These are mine," she said with a laugh. "Get your own. Hi, Carrie. I don't think we've met before, but Arlo has spoken about you and your beautiful daughter."

Carrie smiled at her. "So nice to meet you. And your baby is just precious."

"Thank you. You're going to have to share the recipe with me," Hope said. "I've had some of these before, I think, but yours are way better."

Warmth spread through Carrie. When Arlo put his arm around her shoulders, joy coursed through her. "Thank you. I'm happy to share my recipe with you, for these and everything else I brought."

Ridge jerked to attention, and Hope's eyes widened. "Wait, you brought *more*?" she asked. "Show me."

Carrie brought her closer to the table, trying not to cut in front of anyone who was getting food. She pointed at her platters and explained what each thing was.

"Ridge!" Hope called.

He rushed over.

"We need all of those," she said. "If these leek patties were this good, can you imagine what everything else will taste like?"

"On it," he said.

Tipping his hat to several of the neighbors in line, he rushed to do Hope's bidding. Arlo joined him.

"He really cares about you," Carrie said, nodding toward Ridge.

Hope smiled. "He's wonderful, although I'm sure he's just being polite." Her expression turned pensive. "And so understanding."

Carrie wanted to ask what Hope meant, but she didn't know the woman well enough.

"Arlo is clearly into you, too," Hope added, brightening.

The old Carrie would have been uncomfortable discussing with a stranger whether or not a guy was into her. But Hope wasn't pushy, and Carrie had started the conversation.

"Do you think so?" It couldn't hurt to get an outside perspective. Carrie didn't know much about his past, and she missed the sisterly connection forged by being able to discuss things with Randi.

Hope nodded. "Absolutely. His expression when he looks at you, the way he just casually put his arm around you. And he's lost a lot of the sadness that's been dogging him recently.

"Speaking of which…" Hope put her arm on Carrie's shoulder. "I'm so sorry about Randi and Isaac."

The condolences still stung, but she was starting to get used to them. "Thank you. I'm glad I've been able to help Arlo get through this. He's certainly helped me."

Hope's eyes grew misty, her smile soft. "You two make a wonderful couple."

The men returned, and Hope looked at Ridge appreciatively. "Thank you."

"Anything for you. Can I have some, too, though?"

The four of them laughed.

"Yes, if you insist."

Arlo held out his plate to Carrie. "Take whatever you'd like."

She drew back. "And prevent you from eating? No way."

Ridge chuckled. "She's got your number."

Hope took a bite of the fried pastry frills and closed her eyes. "Oh, my, this is—"

She gasped, dropping her frill and staring straight ahead.

"Hope," Ridge cried. He pulled her against him to shield her. Around them, there were murmurs. Someone found a chair and placed it behind her so Ridge could lower her into it. Someone else moved people out of the way so the four of them could have some space. A third rocked the baby's stroller to keep Evie calm.

Carrie looked on helplessly, gripping Arlo's hand. After

what felt like forever, Hope blinked and burst into tears. She buried her head in Ridge's shoulder, and he held her. The rest of the people in the foyer of the town hall moved away to give her privacy.

Carrie was touched. Seeing how they cared for one of their own, how they made themselves helpful without interfering, impressed her.

When Hope calmed down, Ridge spoke. "Do you want to go home?"

"No. I, uh…remembered things. I was in a house and there were lots of people around." She squinted. "I think it was my house. There were photos of me with the man who'd kissed me, although I still couldn't see his face." She reddened and squeezed Ridge's hand.

"Go on," he said gruffly.

"His face was blurry, but he was familiar. There was a ton of food…" She looked at Carrie, mouth agape. "Your frills were there! I mean, not *yours*, but I think that's what made me remember."

Carrie nodded. "Is that a good thing?" she whispered to Arlo.

"Yes," he said. "She needs to remember. It's the only way she and Ridge can be happy."

"What else did you remember, Hope?" Ridge prompted in a gentle voice.

"Someone came up to me and apologized." She looked at him. "She said my husband was so young."

Hope gasped, and her eyes welled. She blinked her tears away and touched her belly. "I was pregnant."

Carrie, Arlo and Ridge looked at Evie before returning their focus to Hope.

"Did my baby's father die?" Hope sniffled. "I recall that

middle-aged couple coming over to me. They were crying, and they hugged me."

She looked at Ridge, confusion etching her features. "They seemed so nice. But then why am I so afraid of them? Why were they ominous in other memories that I have? Who *are* they?"

"I don't know, but you did great, Hope," Ridge said, rubbing her back.

"When am I going to remember everything?" she moaned.

Someone brought them all water. "Don't rush it, Hope," the person said. "You'll figure it out eventually."

She rested her forehead against Ridge's shoulder. "I hate this," she said.

"I know." His deep voice was soothing.

"Can we go home?"

He stood up and helped Hope to her feet. Arlo and Carrie followed, pushing Evie's stroller as well as Aviva's. Ridge ushered Hope outside and into his truck. When she was settled into the cab of the truck, he shut the door and turned to Arlo.

"Thanks." He looked at his brother, his eyes speaking volumes. Carrie's heart broke for him.

She stood with Arlo as the two pulled away. The luster had been rubbed off the holiday celebration, and Arlo's look of grief was back. But this time, she knew it was for his brother. She wrapped her arm around his waist.

"What can I do for you?" she asked quietly.

He shook his head, stiffening. "I need to be with my brother. Do you mind if I take you home?"

Carrie swallowed. He was doing the right thing by going after his brother, but it hurt that he wouldn't let her comfort him. Her arms almost physically ached to pull him close to her and soothe him. She broke eye contact and nodded, her chest tight.

"Of course."

In silence, they climbed into his truck after getting Aviva settled and drove back to Carrie's house. Arlo said a quick goodbye before backing out of the driveway in a rush, heading toward his brother's house.

"Come on, Vivie, let's go inside."

The rest of the day took forever to pass. Aviva was cranky, Carrie was out of sorts, and her mind kept straying to Arlo and Ridge and Hope.

How awful must it be to lose your memory? Her heart squeezed at the thought of not remembering her sister. She recalled their childhood arguments, playing dress-up together, stealing her clothes when she wasn't looking, and late-night phone calls asking advice about everything. It was bad enough she had started to forget what her voice sounded like. But to completely forget her existence?

And how did Ridge deal with wanting someone who might not be free?

Then there was Arlo. She cared for him. Maybe too much. Her foot bounced. She had a sneaking suspicion she was falling in love with him. Seeing Ridge and Hope together and comparing how Arlo and she were had shown her the similarities between all of four of them, and how she'd grown to depend on him. Was she losing her own independence? Her stomach fluttered. Listening to Hope confirm that Arlo's attention was real and meant something helped to solidify her feelings for him in her mind. But watching him leave without her, not to even consider asking her to join him, hurt. It shouldn't. She was an adult, and if he wanted alone time with his brother, she should understand. And she did. Sort of. But she wished he'd asked her how she felt about it.

She sighed, frustrated with herself. The man had spent almost all his free time with her. He was entitled to as much time with other people as he wanted.

Maybe she was relying on him too much. She'd come to Chatelaine determined to settle her sister and brother-in-law's affairs and take Aviva back to Albuquerque. She'd never intended on forming a relationship with anyone here.

By the time she put Aviva to bed, Arlo still hadn't called. She missed him. Another sign she needed him too much? She sank down in front of the TV, searching for something to watch. Her attention wasn't on anything. She found a Christmas movie on TV and put it on for background noise if nothing else. The movie took place in a small town, making her laugh at the coincidence.

She'd never wanted to live in a small town. Albuquerque had always been her home. She had friends, a thriving Jewish community and amazing restaurants, among other things. Not to mention the anonymity. She missed it.

But, after seeing how everyone behaved today, there was something nice about a town where everyone knew you and looked out for you. That would never have happened in Albuquerque. The people at the celebration today hadn't butted in but had been helpful and respectful of Hope's privacy. Kind of like Myra at the GreatStore the other day with her. They'd even added Hanukkah touches for her. Carrie remembered her conversation with Rita beforehand and made a mental note to thank her if she saw her again.

The truth was, the more she thought about going home

to Albuquerque, the less appealing it was. Despite how much she missed her friends. She'd started to like this town, and after meeting Hope today, she thought they might develop a friendship. Other people at the fair had been friendly, too. Her mind raced. Positives and negatives danced in her brain and overwhelmed her.

There was no Jewish community, but Randi and Isaac had been okay. Maybe she could be, too. Did she want to be? And maybe she could find a Jewish community to join, whether virtually or not too far away. She'd have to look into that soon. *If* she stayed.

Finally giving up on the movie, turned off her phone and went to bed. She'd stop by Hope's in the morning to make sure she was okay. That's what friends did, right? If she wanted her to be her friend, now was the time to act on it.

Arlo sat in Ridge's home, nursing a beer while he waited for his brother to come back. Ridge had gone with Hope to get her settled. The woman was exhausted.

His brother returned and the lines on his face showed his stress. He made a beeline for the fridge, grabbed another beer and plunked down on the overstuffed leather chair across from Arlo. He didn't speak but drank from the bottle in silence.

Arlo let him, knowing full well his younger sibling had a lot to process.

Other than some creaking of floorboards and the faint hum of appliances, the house was silent.

"Let's get some air," Ridge said, rising and striding out of the room.

Arlo followed him onto the porch.

Ridge leaned his forearms on the railing and stared out over the ranch.

"I wish all the memories would just flood back at once," he said.

Arlo paused. With every memory Hope recalled, there was a chance she'd find out her history and have to return to her family. His brother was falling for her. Arlo could see it every time he looked at Hope.

"Why?" he asked carefully. "Aren't you afraid of what you'll find out?"

Ridge took a slug of beer and nodded his head. "Yeah. Terrified. But this not knowing is killing me. Killing *her*. If we knew her story, we could take action one way or another. It's the uncertainty that's leaving us in limbo."

Arlo's heart ached for the two of them.

"I want to be able to help her, regardless of what it means for me, personally." Ridge looked at Arlo, his gaze haunted. "But I can't protect her if I don't know what I'm protecting her from."

"I wish there was something I could do for the two of you."

Ridge took another gulp of beer. "Just be glad you're not in this position. And if you ever are, remember what I said about knowing what you're facing."

They looked out at the property, the millions of stars showing in the clear night. The monochromatic beauty of the place struck Arlo.

"You ever think about Dad?" he asked Ridge.

"All the time. What brought this on?"

"I don't know. The beauty of this place. Dad's dislike of anything having to do with ranch life. How he missed out on all this…" He used his beer bottle to point to the sky.

Ridge nodded. "He missed out on a lot. So did we."

The familiar anger churned in Arlo's belly, and he forced his grip to loosen around the glass bottle.

His brother turned to him. "You know, one of the best things I ever did was make peace with Dad before he died."

Arlo froze.

"Not for any other reason than it freed my mind and brought me some sort of closure."

"So, you just forgave him?" Arlo asked.

"Not exactly. I talked to him and told him why he'd hurt me. I still don't agree with how he treated all of us, but I made my point. It took away a lot of the hurt and put an end to things. I guess you could say it gave me closure."

"And you're okay with him now?"

Ridge leaned his back against the porch railing. "Do I agree with what he did or understand it? No. But talking to him took away the power it held over me."

Thinking over his brother's words, Arlo pressed his hands into the porch railing before looking up at the sky. Sometimes, all he wanted to do was run screaming into the night—his feet pounding the earth, his voice echoing through the open expanse, the wind flying in his face and making his eyes water.

But he kept it all inside, hoping his anger and loss would somehow disappear.

It hadn't happened, yet.

Looking at his brother, he saw the worry lines around his eyes. The man's shoulders were tense with stress. Yet, he looked peaceful. Certainly, more content than Arlo felt. If Ridge could attain that peace despite what was going on with Hope, maybe all wasn't lost for Arlo.

"You know you can talk to me about anything, right?" Ridge asked.

Except he didn't know what Arlo knew. Ridge wasn't aware that their father probably had a second family. He hadn't seen the box of toys with the address written on it.

Arlo didn't want to tell his family what he'd found, not until he knew what it meant. Right now, the knowledge would just shatter their peace of mind. And those of them who'd found it didn't need to lose it so quickly.

"I know," he said. "And I appreciate it. The same goes for you. You and Hope need anything, you let me know."

He finished his beer and hugged his brother. Nothing else needed to be said.

At home, he reached for his phone to call Carrie, but his battery was dead. Swearing under his breath, he plugged it in, then looked at the time. She'd probably be sleeping, and he didn't want to risk waking Aviva. He left it charging on the counter and went to bed.

The next morning, he made coffee and checked his phone.

He frowned. He hadn't spoken to Carrie, and she hadn't contacted him, either. His missed her. Longing to hear her voice, he called her.

"Hey, pretty lady. How are you?" he asked.

There was a small pause before she answered. "How are Ridge and Hope?"

"They're okay," he said, "but you didn't answer my question."

She was quiet.

"Is something wrong, Carrie?"

She sighed. "Yes. Well, no. I'm not sure. I…I think I need some time to myself."

Arlo's stomach rolled. "What's wrong?"

"I'll talk to you later, okay?"

Before he had a chance to respond or even say good-bye, she hung up.

His body tightened, and he jumped up, ready to race over to her house. But she'd said she needed time alone.

It was the last thing he wanted to give her, but echoes of Heath's and Ridge's offers to talk if he wanted, and his own unwillingness to do so, played in his head. As much as it pained him, he had to respect her request.

At least for a little while.

A little while? Arlo scoffed as he looked at his watch for what had to be the fortieth time in three days. He knew it was three days, because he'd picked up his phone at least one hundred times, checking to see if he'd somehow missed a text or call from Carrie. He hadn't.

And the radio-silence was killing him.

Ridge must have gotten all the Fortune patience, because Arlo's ran out. Day three of giving Carrie space was three days too many. And if that made him less understanding, or more reckless, well, he'd work on himself later.

Work. Ha! He'd gotten nothing done.

His eyes stung from sleepless nights, worrying about Carrie, thinking about his father, missing Isaac and wondering if by giving Carrie space he was hurting Aviva.

Oh God, Aviva. Her parents left her. Would her toddler brain think he left her, too?

This was ridiculous. He grabbed his hat, stuffed it on his head and strode out the door. Something was wrong with Carrie, the woman he cared for, and he wasn't waiting any longer. He broke every speed limit in Chatelaine as he rode to Carrie's house, slammed the door and raced onto her porch.

Gripping his hat in his hand so tight he'd probably dent the brim, he rang her doorbell.

Her look of surprise when she answered almost hid the desolation in her gaze. She straightened her shoulders.

"Arlo?"

He'd missed that voice. He'd missed everything about her.

"I know you said you wanted space, but it's been three days. Please don't shut me out any longer."

Her eyes filled, and his heartbeat battered his ribs. He was making her cry.

She blinked before backing up and letting him inside.

He exhaled in relief, and followed her into the kitchen.

He sat down at the island in his kitchen. "Please, Carrie, you can talk to me."

Groaning, her words came out so fast he had to concentrate to understand everything. "I wanted to go with you to Ridge's the other day, but you clearly didn't want me to, which was fine, but I still felt bad. And then I started thinking that maybe I've grown too dependent on you. That led to me reevaluating every part of my personality and all the decisions I've made since Randi died, and I don't know. Everything has changed so fast and I don't want to lose myself as I become a mother, and you've got things to settle in your life, and…"

She paused for breath.

"You asked," she said. She fingered the hem of her shirt, not looking at him. "You probably regret that now."

"Regret you? Never." Sorrow pressed down on him.

"I'm sorry. I never meant to hurt you. I should have included you, and I'm not even sure why I didn't."

She still wouldn't look at him. His heart cracked open.

"I'm used to being alone, I guess," he said. "I don't know why I didn't include you, but I swear there was no intent behind it. And I never, ever meant to make you doubt your ability to take care of yourself. If my trying to help you is doing that…"

Finally, she met his gaze and shook her head.

"It's not. I'm so grateful for your help. I just need to make sure I can stand on my own. I don't mean to be needy. It's so not a good look. And it's a bad lesson for Aviva."

He reached for her hands. "You're the least needy person I know," he said. "It's okay. And if you still want time to yourself, I'll go."

"I think I've had enough," she said, a small smile breaking through. "I've had a lot of time these past three days to let everything settle. I'm less panicky and hopefully more confident."

He reached for her and held her. They stayed that way in silence for several moments. Arlo's stress lessened, his heart beat normally once again, and the dread of being without Carrie lessened.

Finally, he pulled away. "Speaking of needy, though." His voice turned serious. "You've helped me realize something. I think it's time I figured out what's in that box and why my dad was sending it. I don't want to go alone, but I can't ask anyone in my family to come with me. Would you go with me?"

"Of course, I'll go with you." She paused. "You're doing the right thing, you know."

He expelled his breath in a whoosh and rubbed the back of his head. "I hope so. What if I make things worse?"

"How exactly?" she asked.

"Right now, nobody in my family except me knows about the box of toys. It's an easy secret to keep. But if I find proof he had another family, or something equally horrible, I'll have to tell them. I can't keep something like that to myself. And then I'm destroying them."

"You're not responsible for your father, Arlo. And if for some reason, what you find out is truly as bad as you think it might be, we'll figure it out together."

He didn't know if it was the relief of letting out his fears or her response and her use of "we." Maybe it was his conversation with Ridge last night and the fact that he'd slept better after that conversation than he had in months. Whatever the reason, his confidence soared. He could do this.

And knowing Carrie would be with him made it even better.

"When do you want to go?" she asked.

"As soon as possible. Are you free today?"

"I am, but what about Aviva? Are you okay with her coming with us?"

He loved Aviva and spending time with her was never a hardship. But the last thing he wanted to do was introduce her to his father's second family.

"I have an idea, if you're up for it," he said. "Would you be okay if my mom watches her? She loves kids. Heck, she raised all of us."

The silence stretched between them. "Would she even want to? I mean, she doesn't know me or Aviva..."

"We'll leave that up to her. Give me a few minutes to call her and ask, and I'll let you know. Okay?"

When Carrie agreed, Arlo dialed his mom.

"Oh, Arlo, honey, bring her right over. We'll have a grand time while you and your girlfriend spend some time together."

"She's not my girlfriend, Mom." *She wasn't, was she?*

They hadn't discussed their relationship, even though they'd had sex. He frowned. Meaningless sex with a woman like Carrie didn't sit well with him. He wanted something more, and she deserved more. With Aviva gone today, it would be the perfect chance to discuss their relationship. Provided, of course, whatever they discovered wasn't a complete disaster. He groaned silently.

When his mom laughed, he groaned aloud.

"May we drop her off in about an hour?"

"Absolutely. I can't wait to meet her. Aviva, too."

Arlo hung up the phone to the sound of his mother's laughter.

Just great.

"All set with my mom. She'll be ready for us in forty-five minutes."

Now that he was actually planning to solve the mystery, his nerves were on high alert. Multiple times, he wanted to cancel. Or at least put it off until later. But before he knew it, it was time to leave.

"Arwo, I pwetty!" She was dressed as a princess, and he picked her up and tossed her in the air.

"You are the most beautiful princess in all the land," he exclaimed as he put her down.

He looked at Carrie. She looked almost as nervous as he felt, and he grasped her hand. "I promise it's going to be fine."

"I know. I just haven't left her before."

They drove to his mother's home at the main ranch house, which was constructed of weathered light-colored stone with wood finishes and a metal sloped roof. A covered porch extending on either side of the front door had a white railing and six posts.

"I've never seen anything other than the barns and office at the front of the ranch," Carrie said. She craned her neck to see through the front windshield. "I never even knew this was here."

"It's a good thing it is, since my mom can't live in the castle—as I mentioned before, she's renovating it to host guests with a spa and all kinds of amenities. Luckily, this house was also on the property, so she has somewhere to live. Wait until you see inside, and of course, the view from the back," Arlo said. He held open Carrie's door and waited while she took Aviva out of the truck. He followed behind them, watching Carrie grip the toddler's hand.

His mother met them at the door. She was tall and willowy, with blond hair and a quiet, confident air about her. He could tell Carrie immediately felt at ease.

Wendy's face lit up. "Did an actual princess come to visit me today?" She curtsied to Aviva before kneeling down to her level. "I can't wait to spend time with you."

Aviva got shy and hid behind Carrie's leg. Rising, his mom turned to Carrie. "Hi, I'm Wendy. It's so nice to meet you. I was sorry to hear about your sister and brother-in-law."

Carrie shook her hand. "Thank you. And I really appreciate you watching Aviva today. Everything she needs is in her bag. I hope you're not too inconvenienced."

Wendy took the bag from Arlo and gave him a hug. "Are

you kidding? I love playing with little girls, especially one dressed like a princess."

Aviva peeked her head out from behind Carrie's leg.

"Tell me," Wendy said, leading them inside her home. "Does Aviva like cookies?"

Carrie's eyes sparkled. "I don't know." Arlo studied Carrie as she glanced around the front foyer, which led straight into a huge great room, with a stone fireplace and an open stairway leading upstairs.

Aviva nodded, her fingers in her mouth.

"Hmm, I wonder if she'd like to bake some Christmas cookies with me," Wendy said, addressing Carrie.

"Maybe," Carrie said. Arlo noticed Carrie's shoulders relax as she took in the furniture in the room—sturdy wood and leather. It would probably survive her toddler's antics for the day.

Once again, Aviva nodded, and she took a step out from behind Carrie's legs.

Arlo was enjoying watching his mom convince the two-year-old to trust her. She'd always been great with kids, and he loved seeing the joy on her face.

"I was also thinking we could decorate them with frosting and sprinkles. Does she like sprinkles?"

Before Carrie could answer, Aviva said, "Yes."

"You do?" Wendy asked.

Aviva nodded again.

"Then would you like to come with me to make the cookies and decorate them? And I think I have some books that we can read."

Aviva stepped forward and took Wendy's hand. She looked over her shoulder at Carrie.

"Bye, Vivie," Carrie said. "Have fun!"

"Bye, Aviva," Arlo added. "Thanks, Mom!"

He ushered Carrie out the door before the little girl had a chance to get upset or change her mind. Having Carrie to himself made his heart beat a little faster. He always loved spending time with Aviva, but there was something special about having Carrie all to himself.

"I hope you don't mind her decorating Christmas cookies," Arlo said. He placed a hand on the small of her back. It felt right.

"Not at all," Carrie said. She looked behind her before climbing into the truck. "But I hope your mom knows what she's getting into."

Arlo laughed as he started the truck. "Are you kidding? She is so excited to play with Aviva today. She probably should have asked you first, though, about the Christmas thing."

Carrie laid a hand on Arlo's forearm. The heat of her hand permeated his flannel shirt. "I don't mind her learning about other holidays, especially when she's going to be around so many people who celebrate Christmas. I want her to appreciate all of the winter holidays while being proud of celebrating her own."

"Does this mean you're thinking about staying here?" His heartbeat quickened. Spending so much time with Carrie and Aviva brightened his days. His mood was lighter when they were around. He hadn't meant to ask Carrie this question yet, though. He didn't want to push her, but it had just slipped out.

She took her hand away, and his heart dropped. He tried to cover his disappointment by starting the truck and backing out of the driveway. Of course, she wasn't going to stay. She had a life and friends back in Albuquerque.

"Yes," she said. "I'm thinking about it."

His foot pushed harder on the gas pedal at her quiet comment, and he slowed down to normal speed. He couldn't stop the grin from spreading across his face. "I'm glad." He wanted to show her how thrilled he was, but before he had a chance to pull over, she changed the subject.

"How far away do the Fieldses live?" Carrie asked.

Her question doused some of his excitement. "Not far," he said. Which would make it awkward and uncomfortable if they turned out to be his dad's second family.

He scowled.

"You know, this might turn out better than you think," she said, her voice soft.

"Hmm," he grunted. He hated to be so pessimistic, but he didn't see how there could possibly be something good to come out of this. Other than getting rid of a box he was continuously tripping over.

She squeezed his arm once again, and they drove the rest of the way in silence.

Arlo looked one last time at the map on his dashboard, then out the side window at the house he approached. He slowed the truck, his stomach in knots.

"I think that's it," he said, pointing to the modest house set back from the road. It was two stories, with yellow aluminum shingles and a roof that looked like it could use a repair. A tree next to it sported a tire swing, and an old car sat in the driveway.

Arlo shook his head. This was how his dad took care of his second family? He had a hard time believing the man he knew who had been so concerned with appearances could leave people he cared about in a house that clearly needed work.

"You ready?" Carrie asked.

No. "Let's get this over with," he said.

He grabbed the box of toys, waited for Carrie to catch up with him then walked with her to the front door. The cement walkway seemed endless, but too soon, they reached the front door.

Taking a deep breath, he rang the doorbell.

A few moments later, an older woman with gray hair wearing a house dress answered the door. Her face was lined but kind, her eyes inquisitive.

"May I help you?" she asked, peering through the screen door.

"Ma'am, my name is Arlo Fortune. This box was addressed to the wrong house and was returned to my house. I looked up Stevie Fields and came up with this address. I was wondering if maybe it belongs to you or your son?"

The woman's face creased in a wide smile. "That wonderful Casper Windham. Such a generous man. Please, come inside, won't you? I'm Helen, Stevie's grandmother."

Arlo's chest tightened. *Wonderful? Generous?* Was this woman actually talking about his dad? Carrie's hand on his back helped propel him forward, and he entered the dark foyer.

"I just need you to keep your voices down if you don't mind. Little Stevie is upstairs napping. You can leave the box of toys there," she said, pointing to the spot next to the front door. "I'm sure he'll be thrilled with them when he wakes."

She led them into the kitchen, a cheerful room with a big window and peach-colored walls.

"Can I get you something to drink? Coffee, tea, water?"

Arlo was about to refuse. All he wanted was to get out

of here now that he'd delivered the box to his father's other family, but Carrie piped up.

"That would be great. Two coffees, if you have it."

He tensed, ready to refuse, but she caught his gaze and nodded toward a chair at the table. He sat, wondering why he was bothering and what she thought could be gained by remaining here when he had his answer.

Helen knew his father. What else was left to discover?

She brought their coffees, and hers, to the table on a tray, along with sugar, cream and spoons. Then she joined them.

"Casper was your father?" she asked Arlo.

He ground his teeth. He didn't want to tell this woman anything about himself or his family, but the manners that had been drilled into him since he was a child overruled him.

"Yes, ma'am."

She shook her head. "That wonderful man saved my daughter Lynne's life, you know. She's at the hospital getting her chemo treatment. Treatment she couldn't afford until that man came along."

Leaning forward, her eyes glistening with tears, she continued. "While he was a patient at the cancer center, he paid for every patient's care, and arranged for toys to be sent to every patient's kids. Did you know that?"

Arlo shook his head, stunned.

"No, of course not. He swore the hospital to secrecy, of course, but my daughter found out when she went to pay her bill, which is how I know. Stevie and Lynne will have a lovely Christmas now, thanks to your father."

"I...I don't understand." He forced the words from his suddenly parched throat. "My father did this?"

Helen nodded. "He did. He saw how easy it was for him

to get treatment, but how hard it was for others, and know-ing how little time he had, he decided to use his money to help others."

"How do you know?" Arlo asked. "Did you know him?"

"I didn't have the pleasure. But my Lynne did, and she told me how kind and thoughtful he was. You're a lucky man to have had such a father."

Arlo's throat clogged.

The woman's phone rang, and she patted his hand before rising to answer it.

"Are you okay?" Carrie asked, her voice low.

Was he? He had no idea. "How do we get out of here?"

"I'm sorry about that," the woman said. "I'll call them back."

"No, it's really fine," Carrie said. "We've taken up enough of your time."

"Are you sure?"

"Yes. We're so glad to have been able to deliver the toys to Stevie. And thank you for telling us about Mr. Wind-ham."

The older woman bustled about as they headed for the front door. "No problem at all. My condolences to you and your family," she said to Arlo as they exited the house.

Arlo remained silent until they reached the truck.

"Would you rather I drive?" Carrie asked gently.

"No, thanks." He opened her door and then climbed into the driver's seat. Once out of sight of the Fieldses' house, he pulled to the side of the road and bowed his head over the steering wheel. He remained like that, taking deep breaths and sorting his thoughts. Carrie stayed next to him, silent but supportive. Finally, he raised his head.

"Thank you," he rasped. "Thank you for making me do

this and for coming with me and for getting us out of there. I could never have done this on my own."

"You're welcome. How do you feel?"

He mentally probed himself, trying to digest everything the woman had told him, and finally smiled. "Actually, I feel good. Really good. A huge weight has lifted off me. My father wasn't a great dad, but he tried to change and become a better person. And the things he did for the people at the hospital? How amazing was that?"

Cassie's smile brightened her face. "I'm so glad."

He banged the back of his head against the headrest. "I can't believe I'm going to have to tell my brother he was right."

"And me. Don't forget me." Cassie winked.

Arlo's blood heated. "Oh, I couldn't forget you. Ever." He leaned over, slid his hand behind her neck and pulled her toward him. Their mouths met. All of his emotions coalesced into hunger and need and joy, and he put everything into their kiss. Tongues and lips and teeth and the very air they breathed together. She wrapped her arms around him and pressed against him. Their bodies were as close as they could get with the truck console in between them. Their noses bumped as their kiss deepened, until finally, he pulled away.

"I love you, Cassie."

She stared at him, as if memorizing is features.

"You don't have to say it back," he said, his words tumbling out of him. "But I wanted you to know."

Putting a finger over his lips, she hushed him. "I love you, too. I think I have for a while now."

"Even though I messed up the other day?"

She kissed him. "Even though."

She suddenly drew back, concern etched on her face.

"What?" he asked. She'd helped him so much; he wanted to help her, too.

She bit her lip before speaking. "I want to make sure you're not speaking out of some adrenaline rush. You've gone through an emotional rollercoaster, and it's perfectly natural to feel all kinds of things, but when things settle…"

He pulled her closer to him. He liked it better when she was near. "I've loved you for a while. Finding out about my dad maybe hastened my telling you my feelings, but it didn't *create* the feelings."

He caressed her cheek, waiting for her response. After a few moments, she nodded, and he kissed her again.

"We should probably get back," he murmured. "I don't exactly want to have to explain to the cops why I'm pulled over and making out with my girlfriend."

Her cheeks reddened, and she laughed. "Not to mention, you have no idea what I'd say."

Raising an eyebrow, he pulled out onto the road. "Hmm, I may have to rethink this."

She elbowed him. "I dare you."

Their ability to joke in such a carefree manner as he drove them back home filled him with happiness and relief. For the first time since his dad died, he felt as if he was truly free to move on with his life. He pulled his truck into his mom's driveway and parked by the front door.

Carrie was out of the truck before he had a chance to come around and open her door.

"Mom, we're back!" he yelled as they entered her home. He inhaled, the smell of baked cookies permeating the house. "And something smells delicious!"

"Cawwy, Arwo, wook!" The toddler's feet pounded on the tile floor, and she plowed into their legs a moment later.

Carrie lifted her in her arms. "Hello," she said.

"Wook at my cookie." She held out the cookie, and Carrie opened her mouth wide.

"Oh, my goodness, it's beautiful!"

"Twy it?"

She stuck the cookie in Carrie's mouth before she had a chance to answer. Arlo laughed as Carrie took a quick bite and chewed.

"It's delicious. You did such a good job."

Aviva leaned toward Arlo, and he took a bite as well.

"Yummy," he said.

He walked with Carrie and Aviva to the kitchen. It was situated in a nook on one end of the great room, with an island counter in the center, a brick backsplash over the stove, white marble counters and stainless-steel appliances. Wendy had set up an area at the island for Aviva to sit and decorate.

"There's my best helper," Wendy said. She walked over and kissed Arlo on the cheek and smiled at Carrie. "She was such a great girl, and we had so much fun, didn't we?"

Aviva bobbed her head, making her blond curls bob.

Wendy did a double take. "Arlo, you look happy." Her voice was filled with shock.

Pain over the worry he'd caused his mother stabbed him. "I am, and I'd like to tell the family why." He looked around at the lack of Christmas decorations.

"How about we have the family over tomorrow to decorate, and I'll tell everyone what I learned today?"

She frowned. "You mean I have to wait?"

He nodded.

She looked between him and Carrie and then back again. "Okay." She smiled. "I'm so glad to see you happy, I'd probably agree to anything."

Arlo texted his siblings in their group chat, before rubbing his hands together in mock glee. "Good to know."

Chapter Eight

The next day, Arlo's siblings poured into Wendy's house, astonishing Carrie with their boisterous behavior.

The brothers—Nash and Ridge—and the sisters—Dahlia, Sabrina and Jade—clapped Arlo's back, hugged and kissed him, and exclaimed over his complete change in attitude. Even the siblings' significant others noticed.

Carrie appreciated it as well. The cloud hanging over his head had disappeared, lightening his voice, straightening his shoulders and bringing into sharp focus all the traits she'd come to love about him—his eagerness, devotion and compassion for others.

And the Christmas decorations? Wow.

The Fortune family took decorating seriously. Even Arlo, who'd expressed no interest prior to this, was eager to trim his mother's tree.

Carrie was a little overwhelmed. She and Aviva sat on one of the chairs in Wendy's living room and watched the bustle of people. The room was at the back of the house—and as Arlo had warned, the back of the house was the most impressive, with huge windows overlooking the lake and a multilevel deck and patio. The living room had another fireplace—there were several in Wendy's home—with a brandy-colored mantle and turquoise marble. The floors were made of gray stone, and the walls were painted a similar shade of turquoise as the fireplace marble. White trim outlined the windows and molding. The effect was dramatic but warm. Their Christmas tree filled a back corner of the room. As each of Wendy's kids and their loved ones had arrived, they'd helped to carry a box or two of decorations into the living room. Or they'd brought their own. By the time everyone was present, Carrie was pretty sure bringing a lively two-year-old with her had been a mistake. There was no way she wasn't going to get into everything and probably break something.

"Okay, Arlo, we've been patient long enough," Wendy said once everyone had settled into the oversize golden velvet sofas. "What did you want to tell us?"

Carrie squeezed his hand, and he rose, walking over to the fireplace and looking around the room.

"Almost two months ago, the mail carrier brought a box that had been misaddressed back to the ranch. It was from Dad, addressed to Stevie Fields. Inside the box were toys."

Confusion marred everyone's faces.

"Who is Stevie Fields?" Dahlia asked.

"And why was Dad sending toys to someone?" her twin, Sabrina, added.

"I had the same questions," Arlo said. "I was convinced Dad had a second family somewhere, and I didn't want to tell any of you because I didn't want to upset you."

Wendy gasped. "Arlo!"

He held up his hand. "I was wrong," he acknowledged. "About many things. First, I should never have kept the news from all of you. It was too much to bear alone. I talked to Isaac about it, and he tried to convince me I was wrong and should find out more information. We argued, I refused and then he died."

"Oh, gosh," Jade said. "I wish you'd told us."

He nodded. "Again, I was wrong. Heath suggested I tell you all—not that he knew anything, just the general idea of a secret I was keeping—and I wanted to, but I didn't know how. Thanks to Carrie and Ridge and a few other things that unfolded, I decided to find out once and for all what was going on."

He took a deep breath. "Dad did *not* have a second family. He was paying for patients' chemo at the hospital who were going through treatment at the same time he was, and he was delivering toys to their children so they could have a festive holiday."

The room went silent. Through the reflection in the windows, Carrie saw everyone digesting the information. And she stared at them in astonishment. Not that they shouldn't be shocked, but the noise level prior to this had been so loud, their ability to quiet down surprised her. But it didn't last. Chaos erupted. She watched as everyone spoke at once, disbelief and confusion covering their faces like masks during Purim celebrations. Arlo answered the questions flying at him in quick succession. And finally, their faces brightened.

"Dad had a change of heart," Nash said. "I'll be darned."

Ridge's face shone. "I knew it." His voice wasn't loud, but still, the room heard him.

As one, they turned to Wendy. She had remained silent, and it was to her that everyone seemed to look to for the official conclusion.

She held the room with her silence, until finally, she spoke. "Your father was far from a perfect man. But I'm glad that, in the end, he returned to the person I first fell in love with. I hope all of you are able to make peace with him now, in time for the holidays."

They all murmured their agreement.

She turned to Arlo. "Thank you for trying to spare us more pain," she said. "I know it wasn't easy. The toll it took on you." She walked over to him and took his face between her hands. "Do not ever feel you have to do that again."

Everyone rose, hugged Arlo, and continued to decorate their mother's home for Christmas. Dahlia festooned the fireplace with fir boughs and tiny bells. Sabrina began decorating the tree. Jade, Hope and Nash's fiancée, Imani, hung wreaths and mistletoe on all the windows. Nash and Ridge, as well as the other men, went outside to begin stringing the lights on the house and the deck.

Wendy came over to Carrie and took her hands. "You have brought me the best Christmas gift of all. My son's happiness."

Her hands in the older woman's, Carrie felt tears come to her eyes. "The feeling is mutual."

"I hope you'll join us on Christmas Eve for our book exchange," Wendy said. "We'd love to have you share in our tradition."

Carrie inhaled, surprised but also delighted by the invitation. "I'd love to, thank you."

"Wonderful. Arlo will have to give you all the details."

After they hugged again, Wendy's face brightened. Putting her arm around Carrie's shoulders, she turned to the group. "Sleigh ride, anyone?"

Carrie frowned. "Sleigh ride?" She looked toward the bank of windows. It was a clear night, with the moon shining off the lake. "I never knew it snowed out here."

Arlo's mom squeezed her shoulders. "No, honey, this is Texas. We don't get snow down here. We do, however, love Christmas, and I thought it would be fun to offer our guests a Texas-style sleigh ride."

With the rest of the family clamoring to go, Carrie nodded. She made eye contact with Arlo. Striding over to her, he pulled her away from Wendy, and the two of them followed the rest of the family outside.

"Need a rescue?" he whispered in her ear.

Just being in his arms was enough for her. "No, but I'm curious about what your mom has planned."

Outside were two hay wagons, dressed in fir boughs, red ribbons and bells. Four horses, two per wagon, were harnessed, and two ranch hands sat in the driver's seat, wearing Stetsons with holly and bows.

Carrie smiled. "Now I get it."

The family divided themselves between the two wagons, pulling red and green plaid blankets over their laps, sitting on bales of hay and drinking thermoses of hot cocoa the ranch hands had offered.

Carrie snuggled against Arlo as she kept a protective arm around Aviva. "Where are we riding to?"

The ranchers clicked their tongues, and the horses began to trot, the bells on their harnesses jingling.

"Around the ranch, along the lake and back. Are you ready for some good, old-fashioned Christmas-y fun?"

"More than ready!" Carrie murmured. "And the more time I get to spend with you, the better."

He bent his head to kiss her, their mouths coming together and sending shards of warmth through Carrie.

"I could get used to this," he whispered.

"Me, too."

* * *

The next evening, after spending the day tackling all the ranch business he'd ignored, Arlo returned to his house, alone. Carrie was with Dahlia and Sabrina at Jade's house for the sisters' annual Christmas cookie baking extravaganza in preparation for the annual cookie contest. She was showing them how to make *bimuelos* and fried pastry frills. He was thrilled she'd been accepted into the family so easily. Tomorrow, he'd take her over to Remi's Reads to purchase books for his family's Christmas Eve exchange. He sat on his back deck, staring up at the stars. Perseus twinkled in the northern sky. For the first time in months, he was at peace. He didn't mind being alone because he wasn't uncomfortable with where his thoughts would take him.

And those thoughts were filled with Carrie and Aviva. Carrie had given him his soul back. She'd shown him that it was okay to have faith in the goodness of people. That not everyone was going to disappoint you. And thanks to her, he'd come to terms with his relationship with his father. He'd learned that although the man might not have been the best father, he wasn't a horrible person. He'd finally been able to forgive the man. And he'd been able to appreciate the joy in the world around him again.

Carrie was smart and sexy. He admired her ability to persevere despite horrible tragedies. And she let him help her, despite her independence. He knew how hard that was. God knew, he had trouble leaning on people, too. But she'd let him in, confided in him and showed him how to be a better person in the process.

And Aviva? She was a joy. He'd play animals with her every day for the rest of his life if she'd let him.

The rest of his life?
Yes.

He walked down toward the lake, thinking about the adorable toddler. He couldn't wait to share Hanukkah and Christmas with her. Since Hanukkah started on Christmas day this year, she was going to be totally overwhelmed with presents and sugar and fun, and he looked forward to experiencing the joy and the meltdowns. Aviva loved helping to decorate—his mother's tree had gobs of tinsel unevenly placed thanks to her—and the Christmas cookies had been a hit. Tomorrow night, he'd celebrate Hanukkah with her and Carrie, followed immediately by Christmas. If possible, he was more excited than Aviva was. Like most toddlers, she'd loved the wrapping paper and boxes as much as the toys he'd gotten her, but watching her face in the glowing candlelight had filled him with awe. He couldn't wait to share in her traditions as well.

At the shoreline, he stared at the calm water, the stars reflecting off the surface, and marveled at how lucky he was. He sent a quick message of thanks to Isaac. "You were right," he said softly. Feeling more at peace, he turned toward his home, but stopped when movement on the lake caught his eye. Two people, taking an evening stroll. He smiled. If things worked out like he hoped, one day that would be him and Carrie. And then he squinted. The woman looked like his mother. Same build, same hairstyle. When he heard her laughter, he was positive. But who was she walking with? He squinted again. At night, everything took on a monochromatic hue. But just as he was about to give up, the couple walked beneath one of the lights along the lake. The man wore a gray Stetson.

Hmm. Lots of men around these parts wore Stetsons,

so it was anyone's guess who her gentleman companion could be.

Arlo paused. The idea of his mother in love was new to him. On the one hand, as her son, he really didn't want to consider romantic love and his mother with the same brain, much less in the same thought. But on the other hand, no one deserved a second chance at love more than she did. If she and her suitor were happy, he certainly wasn't going to interfere.

Nor was he going to stay out here watching them. They deserved privacy.

Turning quickly, he walked back to his house.

Carrie and Aviva once again walked into total chaos when they arrived at Wendy's home for the Fortune family's Christmas Eve celebration. Holiday music played through a piped-in sound system, fir boughs, red balls and bells festooned every doorway, banister and mantle, and twinkle lights glowed everywhere.

Arlo met her at the door.

"Welcome, pretty lady," he said. He leaned forward and gave her a kiss. His lips were warm and firm, and she barely had time to notice anything else before he pulled away and pointed upward.

"Mistletoe."

She smiled. "Is that the only reason you kissed me?"

His eyes glowed, and one corner of his mouth turned up. "No, that's the reason I kissed you now."

Aviva leaned toward him and pursed her lips. "Me kiss, me kiss."

Laughing, he kissed her forehead before taking her in his arms and helping them off with their coats.

"Come on inside," he said.

With his hand on the small of Carrie's back, he led her into the living room, where the enormous Christmas tree stood in the corner. Large windows faced what she knew to be the lake, although at night they reflected the family party.

She'd been here last week with Arlo, had even been part of the decorating, but somehow, tonight, everything looked a little overwhelming.

Luckily, Arlo and his family put her at ease. Ridge and Hope gave her a hug as they entered the room. "Happy Hanukkah a little early," Ridge said to Carrie.

"Ridge tells me it starts tomorrow night?" Hope continued.

Carrie nodded, touched they'd remembered. "It does. Merry Christmas to you both."

"Thank you. Are you doing anything special to celebrate?" the auburn-haired woman asked.

"I was telling Arlo we usually have a big family meal on the last night. I'd love you two to join us if you're free."

The four of them pulled out their phones and consulted their calendars.

"Hey, you guys," another of the men said. "No playing on your phones."

"We're not playing, Nash," Arlo said. "Hi, Imani." He gave his brother a pat on the back and hugged Nash's fiancée.

"Well, definitely no business talk," she said. "It's Christmas."

Carrie smiled. "I'm sorry… It's my fault. I invited them to my *merenda*—my Hanukkah dinner—and they were checking their calendars. I'd love for you all to come as well." She looked at Arlo. "Actually, your entire family is invited if they're free."

She smiled at Arlo's siblings and their partners.

"Twee," Aviva said, pointing to the corner of the room.

The three of them walked over to the Christmas tree. With a gold star on top, ornaments both handmade and store-bought, twinkling white lights and silver garlands, Carrie thought it was beautiful.

She also thought it was way too fragile for a two-year-old to play with. Or touch. Or even breathe near.

But then she saw the brightly wrapped gifts beneath the tree—the ones she and Aviva brought included—and all thoughts of staying in the same room fled. She did not want to be known as the "tree destroyer."

Arlo must have realized her concerns, because he gently told Aviva not to touch while showing her everything she wanted to see.

Wendy walked up to them with a big smile. She kissed both Arlo and Carrie. "I'm so glad you are here."

Taking Aviva from Arlo's arms, she played with the toddler's blond curls. "Hello, my special cookie helper! Would you like to see the cookies you made? I put them out especially for you."

Aviva nodded and happily went with Wendy to the dining area, where a large table with a red-and-green tablecloth was arranged with lots of Christmas treats.

"Relax," Arlo whispered. "She'll be fine."

"I'm not worried about Vivie," Carrie said. "I'm worried about all your Christmas decorations being destroyed by a two-year-old Grinch."

Arlo laughed, his deep baritone flooding Carrie with

warmth. "With everyone who is here to keep an eye on things, the decorations are perfectly safe."

"If you say so." She wasn't convinced.

Dahlia and her husband, Rawlston, walked over and greeted them, interrupting their conversation. "Now that you're here, we can do our gift exchange."

Carrie's heart beat a little faster. She'd asked Arlo what to get for everyone, and he'd told her books. But that was all he'd said, and what if he was wrong?

He squeezed her hand, and everyone sat on the blue tufted sofas. They were as comfortable as they looked, and Carrie reminded herself to talk to Wendy the next time she decided to redecorate her house.

Jade rose and addressed the room, her fiancé, Heath, looking at her lovingly. "Since we have a bunch of newcomers this year—" she returned Heath's loving look "—we want everyone to understand the Fortune Christmas Eve tradition. Crazy Christmas gifts aren't necessary. Most of us have everything we need, and who needs that pressure?"

Everyone laughed.

"So, on Christmas Eve, we do a book exchange." She held up her hand as people started to speak. "However, we wouldn't be this family if we didn't do things a little differently. So, everyone go take the presents you brought and come find your seat."

Carrie was totally confused but did as she was told. With a pile of wrapped gifts on her lap, she waited for Jade to continue.

"Everyone ready?"

They all nodded.

"Okay, Mom, you go first."

Wendy took the top present on her pile and handed it to

Arlo. He unwrapped it, smiled and held it up. It was a hard-cover of Charles Dickens's *A Christmas Carol*. Everyone oohed and ahhed, and then Dahlia spoke up.

"Sorry, brother dear, I want that." She walked over and plucked it from his hands.

Carrie and the other guests who were unfamiliar with the Fortune tradition looked at each other in confusion.

"Yup, when you unwrap the gift, anyone can steal it from you. If your book is stolen, you get to pick again. But you can only steal a book if you don't currently have one, so choose wisely."

Arlo picked a book off Dahlia's pile, unwrapped it and held it up again. This time, it was an Agatha Christie mystery.

"This is going to be great," he said. He pulled the top present from his stack and handed it to Rawlston, who laughed when he opened it.

"Love Letters of Great Men," he said and showed it to the room. "A few months ago, I might have hated this book." He looked at Dahlia. "But now, I love it."

When no one moved to steal it, Rawlston took the top package off his stack and handed it to Imani.

"I'm not sure whether to be scared or excited." She chuckled as she opened the package. She held up *What To Expect, The Toddler Years*.

As she started to laugh, Carrie said, "Oh, wait, I want that!"

The two women pretended to argue, until Carrie said, "I'll let you borrow it as soon as I'm done."

Imani agreed and picked a book from Carrie's stack. *"Sephardic Heritage Cookbook?* Okay, Carrie officially wins the best books prize," Imani cried. "I can't wait to try these." She pulled the top book from her stack and handed it to Zane.

He unwrapped the gift and held it against his chest. "Nope, not trading."

"Hey, that's not part of the rules, Zane," Jade scolded. "Come on, let us see."

He glared at everyone in the room before displaying *1000 Places To See Before You Die*.

"I think Zane gets a pass on this one," Wendy said. "Because it is absolutely perfect. Imani, great job."

Imani bowed her head and then rose at the sound of a baby crying. "If you'll excuse me for a minute…"

Imani and Nash took their son into the other room.

"Let's pause the book exchange until they get back," Jade suggested, and everyone agreed.

Carrie leaned forward. "How long have you done this book exchange?"

"Since the kids were little," Wendy said, a faraway look in her eye. "The kids were always so excited about Christmas, and it was a fun way to help them deal with the excitement before Santa arrived."

Squeezing Aviva, who'd returned to her side and crawled onto her lap, Carrie nodded. "I love the tradition. My friends and I used to do something similar at Hanukkah parties in college, but with gag gifts."

Heath's gaze brightened, and he looked down at his pile of books. "That could be a lot of fun, even if we did it with books."

Shaking her head, Wendy demurred. "Absolutely not! That sounds like a perfect activity for you all to do without me in another place at another time." She grinned. "I'm really better off not participating in your sense of humor."

Everyone laughed, and Imani and Nash returned to the room.

"That was fast," Wendy added. "Everything okay?"

"It wasn't a full-blown meltdown so we're okay," Imani said. "But let's continue before one of those happens."

"Good idea," Arlo said. "Who's next?"

Zane pulled a book off the pile on his lap and handed it to Jade. "You are."

The family continued the book exchange until everyone had received, stolen, taken back and laughed at all the books. By the end, each person had a mixed pile of books to read.

"Now remember," Wendy said. "Read the ones you like and donate the ones you don't. Remi's Reads is collecting donations to send to troops overseas, so anything you don't want, someone else will."

Carrie looked around at the group of people. By all accounts, they had everything. Wealth, success and happiness. And still they found ways to help others. Even with a Christmas Eve tradition.

"What are you thinking?" Arlo asked, leaning toward her. They headed over to the dining table that was piled with all the holiday cookies they'd made.

"Just about how nice this tradition is," she said, as she took her plate and picked out a variety of confections. She saw the dreidel cookies she'd made and loved how Wendy had included them.

"Hot chocolate, egg nog and peppermint tea, with alcohol to add on if you'd like, is on the counter," Wendy said.

Carrie turned to everyone who had gathered around for their Christmas Eve snacks. "While you're all here, I want to make sure to invite all of you to my Hanukkah *merenda* on the eighth night of the holiday. I'd love to have you join me and Aviva for our celebration."

Arlo hugged her to him. "That's a lot of people," he said as they walked to one of the large sofas. "You sure you want to do that?"

"Absolutely." She smiled at him. "You've shared your holiday, and I want to share mine."

Chapter Nine

About a week later, Carrie put the finishing touches on her dining table, getting it ready for the *merenda* that evening. She'd invited Rita from the bookstore, as well as the entire Fortune family and their partners. Everyone was bringing a dish to share for the potluck celebration. She appreciated how open they were about learning about her traditions, and they'd been excited to pull recipes from some of the cookbooks she'd given them on Christmas Eve. When the sun set, they'd light the menorah.

Taking a step back, she surveyed the room, taking in the white tablecloth, blue and white napkins, and blue and silver china she'd found in Randi's closet. The menorah held pride of place on the table in front of the window, where it had stood for each of the previous seven nights. Aviva loved watching the candles flicker.

She'd hung some multicolored foil Hanukkah decorations from the ceiling—mostly dreidels—and she'd sprinkled chocolate gelt wrapped in foil on the surfaces in the room.

Delicious smells wafted from the kitchen, and she went back in to check that nothing was burning, bubbling over, or bursting into flame.

Aviva sat on the floor in a red dress playing with Arlo's dreidel.

Carrie wiped her hands on a towel so as not to mess up her jeans and pink sweater. She couldn't wait for him to get here. Since they'd uncovered his dad's secret and Arlo had finally found peace, their life had settled into a comforting routine. They each worked during the day and then spent their meals together in the evenings. Sometimes at Arlo's, most times at Carrie's since it was easier with Aviva. He'd occasionally spend the night at her house as well. But for the last few days, she'd barely seen him. He'd said he was working on something for her, a Hanukkah surprise, so Carrie didn't push.

But she missed him. Missed being wrapped in his strong arms. Missed their quiet discussions before they fell asleep. Missed his company.

Her doorbell rang, startling her out of her musings. Aviva jumped up and ran to the door, and Carrie followed. Guests weren't due to arrive for another half hour, but when she peeked through the peephole, she smiled.

"Arlo." She wrapped her arms around him and kissed him. "I missed you," she said.

"I missed you, too," he murmured, nuzzling her neck.

"Arwo!"

"Neigh, neigh," he said, getting down on all fours and tossing his head. His shoulder muscles bulged through his white button-down.

Aviva giggled and climbed on his back. "Wide, hawsey, wide!"

He galloped her around the foyer, before depositing her on the bottom stair and rising to his full height.

"The place looks great," he said. "What can I help you with?"

Carrie shook her head. "I'm all set."

"Good, that gives me a chance to talk to you before everyone arrives." He pulled an envelope out of his shirt pocket and handed it to her.

"Oh, no. Not another mystery," she moaned. The envelope was made of heavy stock, like an invitation or a piece of stationery.

He laughed. "Well, kind of, but that's not why I'm giving it to you. Open it, please."

His intense look made her shiver. She lifted the flap of the envelope and peered inside. She pulled out an embossed invitation which invited Arlo and a guest, as well as any children or pets, to dinner.

She turned the envelope over. There was no return address.

"Who is this from?"

He shrugged. "I have no idea. It's not the first I've received. Back in July, my siblings and I all received plain invitations to a wedding to be held next month at the ballroom in the town hall."

Carrie frowned. "Oh, wait, that's where the gingerbread houses were, right?"

He nodded. "Yeah. No idea if they're part of it, since we don't even know who the bride or groom is or, really, anything about the wedding."

"You're kidding!"

"Nope. Not only that, in August, we all received texts asking our opinions on bride and groom outfits. Then we were asked to pick a quote that captures how we feel about love and family."

Carrie squeezed his hand. "What quote did you pick?"

Arlo shifted in his chair, clearly uncomfortable. He sighed, and after a bit more prodding from her, finally shared a passage from his favorite book that summed up the true meaning of family, friendship and forever love.

"I love that quote," Carrie said softly.

He smiled. "Anyway, I was hoping you'd be my plus-one?"

"Of course," she said, kissing him again. "I'd love to. You seem to get yourself caught up in a lot of surprises."

"Do you mind them?" He pulled her into his arms.

Mind them? If they let her be with Arlo, she'd welcome them forever. "No."

"In that case…" He kissed her again before dropping to one knee.

She gasped.

"Carrie, our relationship has progressed from one surprise to the next. Not all the surprises have been good ones, but all of them have been better with you by my side. The more we're together, the less I ever want you to leave. You and Aviva are such a wonderful part of my life. Would you spend the rest of yours with me? Will you marry me?"

"Oh, Arlo, yes." Her eyes filled with tears, but this time, they were happy ones. "You've shown me what love truly means. That as long as we're together, we can handle anything. That the only place I belong is by your side. You're my home, and there's nowhere I'd rather be than with you."

He slid a sparkling diamond ring on her finger right before Aviva ran over and hugged him.

Carrie knelt next to both of them and hugged them tight. She'd come to Chatelaine, Texas, to help out her sister, right before being plunged into the deepest despair she'd ever suffered. And through it all, Arlo had been by her side, even through all of his own troubles. Together, they were a family, despite the wrenches thrown in front of them, despite their differences. They were stronger together than apart, and Carrie couldn't think of anyone she'd rather spend her life with.

"I love you, Arlo. So, so much."

"I love you, Carrie."

"I wuv you, too!" Aviva piped up, to peals of laughter.

At that moment, Carrie's doorbell rang. She shot a questioning look at Arlo, who nodded. She rose and answered the door. Hope, Ridge and Wendy stood on her porch, holding platters covered in foil.

"Come in." She smiled at all of them as she made way for them to enter her foyer. As everyone greeted her and Arlo and Aviva, Rita and Doris arrived as well. The din in her foyer was happy and loud, something she'd missed after all this time.

They all traipsed into the kitchen with their contributions for the *merenda*. As Carrie directed everyone where to put their dishes, she tried to figure out how to tell everyone she and Arlo were engaged. Maybe he wouldn't want to tell his family now while others were present?

Just then, Hope gasped, and Carrie rushed over to where Ridge was pulling a kitchen chair out for the distraught woman. He placed a hand on her shoulder.

"What's wrong?" Concern marred his boyish features.

Hope took a deep breath. Her face reddened as she looked around the room at all of the worried guests.

"I'm sorry," she said. "I didn't mean to cause another scene."

Carrie spoke up. "You didn't. We just want to make sure you're okay."

Ridge flashed her a grateful look, and sympathy filled her.

Hope nodded. "I had another flashback. I don't know,

maybe it was seeing everyone carrying things in here that prompted it, but I was carrying Evie and my baby bag. I was running for the bus—" she frowned "—I think it was near the LC Club and I thought I saw the middle-aged couple again. I missed the bus and then it was dark. I knew I needed to find shelter and it felt like I was walking forever until I found a barn." She looked up at Ridge. "And that's all I remember until I woke up with you looking over me."

"I guess we finally know what happened," Arlo murmured.

"But why was I running away from home?" Hope asked. "I still have so many questions."

Ridge knelt in front of her. "I know, honey. But as your memory comes back, we're putting pieces together, and at least we're getting closer to finding out what happened. I'll protect you from whatever happened. I promise."

"We all will." Carrie's guests murmured their assent, reminding her once again how wonderful all these people were.

"Do you want to go rest?" she asked. "You're welcome to lay down upstairs."

Hope shook her head, seeming to get ahold of herself. "No, I want to enjoy myself and spend time with all of you. You've all been so kind to me."

Carrie smiled at her. "I'm glad to have you here, and I'd like to think we can be friends."

Hope nodded. "I'd like that."

"Good." She looked out the window. "I hate to rush everyone, but the sun is setting. If everyone can join me in the living room, it's time to light the menorah."

She led them into the room, lifted up Aviva and had her pick out the candles and the order in which to place them.

Of course, the child wanted lots of red ones. Before lighting, she turned to her guests.

"It's so nice to celebrate Hanukkah with all of you," she said. "Aviva and I have lit the menorah each of the other seven nights right here, using the center candle as the 'helper' and adding one candle each night. But tonight, we light all eight of them. But first, we recite a prayer…"

She sang the Hebrew blessings and then guided Aviva's hand while they lit the candles together. When they finished, Arlo turned out the lights in the room so they could all see the beautiful menorah fully lit. The candlelight glowed on Aviva's cheeks. The hush of their family and friends marked the occasion as special. Everyone remained silent for a moment. Then Arlo turned on the lights again, and the talking resumed.

"Such a beautiful tradition," Wendy said.

"Thank you so much for sharing it with us," Hope added. Ridge nodded in agreement.

"Thank *you* for joining me," Carrie told them. "It makes Hanukkah special when we can celebrate together."

"And tonight is even more special," Arlo added. He rose, sending a questioning glance her way. Her cheeks heated, and she couldn't resist the smile that spread across her face.

"Yes, it is."

He joined her at the head of the table. "We're getting married!" he announced. He kissed her, speaking as their lips touched. "I love you."

"I love you, too."

The whoops and congratulatory calls filled the air, and everyone swarmed the two of them.

The women cried happy tears, and Ridge slapped his

brother on the back. Then he hugged Carrie. "Welcome to the family."

And finally, she found her home.

* * * * *

Don't miss
Fortune's Mystery Woman
by New York Times *bestselling author Allison Leigh,*
the next installment in the new continuity
The Fortunes of Texas: Fortune's Secret Children
On sale January 2024, wherever
Harlequin books and ebooks are sold!

And catch up with the previous titles in the series:

Fortune's Secret Marriage
by Jo McNally

Nine Months to a Fortune
by New York Times *bestselling*
author Elizabeth Bevarly

Fortune's Faux Engagement
by Carrie Nichols

A Fortune Thanksgiving
by Michelle Lindo-Rice

Available now!

HARLEQUIN
Reader Service

Enjoyed your book?

Try the perfect subscription for Romance readers and get more great books like this delivered right to your door.

See why over 10+ million readers have tried Harlequin Reader Service.

Start with a Free Welcome Collection with free books and a gift—valued over $20.

Choose any series in print or ebook. See website for details and order today:

TryReaderService.com/subscriptions